A Vineyard Celebration

A Vineyard Sunset Series

Katie Winters

Chapter One

The best day of Amanda's life was also the worst for her career. She went into labor and lost her sense of self in one fell swoop.

Amanda felt her first contraction at the Sheridan House. She'd heaved herself over a cushioned porch chair with a bowl of popcorn and a large bottle of water to watch the seagulls caw over the sound. Max, now three, terrorized the yard in front of the porch, whacking anything he could with a stick, including trees, stones, and the porch railing. Amanda had agreed to watch him while Audrey finished a big story for a magazine upstairs. Being the size of a beached whale meant she couldn't be as hands-on as Max wanted. "Auntie Amanda!" he called many times. "Come play!"

That was when the contraction shot through her. It was like someone reached into her body and squeezed as tightly as they could. She gasped and winced and waited. Although she'd already read sixteen baby books about labor, delivery, and the first few weeks of childcare, her mind went blank. She wasn't ready for this!

Audrey heard her from upstairs and burst out through the back door. "Is it happening?"

The contraction faded just then. More were around the corner, though. Amanda could sense it.

"What was it they said?" Amanda muttered. "We go to the hospital when the contractions are how far apart?"

Why couldn't Amanda remember a single fact about this huge momentous occasion? She was Amanda Harris. She'd graduated at the top of her glass at Rutgers Law School. She could speed-read at a 90 percent comprehension rate. Why had this biological process destroyed her intellect?

Audrey wasn't used to Amanda not knowing things. "Um? I think like five minutes apart?"

"Didn't you already do this? Why don't you remember?" Amanda asked, then hated herself for snapping. Fear was a horrible emotion. It made you into a monster.

Immediately, she added, "I'm sorry. I'm just scared."

"Don't worry about it."

Audrey hurried down the steps to pick up Max and take him back inside to prop him in front of the television. She returned with Amanda's favorite baby book about labor and delivery, Fig Newtons, and her cell phone.

"You should keep working," Amanda rasped. "You have a deadline."

"So do you," Audrey shot back with a laugh. "And yours is more important than mine."

A few minutes after the third contraction rattled through Amanda, she got ahold of her husband. Sam was the manager at the Sunrise Cove Inn. Although it was only April, tourist season loomed over them, ever approaching, and he had many plans for the upcoming season that kept him at the inn for long hours. *"I want to get as much done as I can before the baby comes,*" he'd said many times.

When Sam learned Amanda was in labor, his voice jumped up an octave and fell back down. "Okay! Okay. It's okay. We're going to have a baby, Amanda! I love you so much!"

Amanda beamed and winced and brought her hands into fists. This was what they wanted. They were building their family.

"I'll wrap everything up here and come pick you up," Sam promised.

Amanda thanked him, put down the phone, then squeezed Audrey's hand so hard during the next contraction that Audrey turned the color of a cucumber.

"Dang, Amanda. Do you lift weights?" Audrey quipped as the contraction faded.

Amanda sputtered with relief after the wave of pain. "You better be glad I don't."

Up at the hospital, Amanda was given a beautiful room with a view of the Vineyard Sound. It was early afternoon, and the April light shimmered across the water and lit up the swell of grass outside. Nurses buzzed in and out to make sure she was comfortable and checked her stats. Sam was all set up beside her, smiling goofily between contractions. Amanda's mother, Susan, arrived not long after that, looking more frantic than Amanda had seen her in years. It took a great deal to rattle Susan Sheridan. Childbirth was no joke. Amanda was a realist, and she knew things went wrong all the time. She also knew that because it was her first, labor could last ten, fifteen, or even up to twenty-four hours. She tried to think of it like a marathon. She had to pace herself.

Aunt Christine and Aunt Lola came up to the

hospital soon after. They were ladened with snacks and drinks, smiling prettily. Christine carried her toddler Mia on her hip and said very nice things about labor, like, "It'll be a breeze for you, Amanda. You're so strong." Amanda didn't believe her at all, but it was still nice to hear. The overwhelming love and support in the Sheridan family was unmatched elsewhere. Sometimes, it was difficult for Amanda to remember the time "before." Before Susan returned to Martha's Vineyard to make amends with Grandpa Wes, they'd learned Grandpa Wes hadn't been the one to have anything to do with Grandma Anna passing so long ago. Before the family had fallen into the warm embrace of countless dinners, celebrations, weddings, and births.

Sometime before six that evening, Amanda did something stupid. She looked at her phone.

In her inbox was an official-looking email from the Massachusetts Board of Bar Overseers. Amanda frowned. Was this really the time to read this?

"Your brother sends his love," Amanda's mother said from the window, where she sorted a few bouquets that others had brought to brighten up the room. "I'm sure they'll come out to visit this month. Everyone will want to meet the new baby!"

Amanda's heart thudded. "Yeah. Can't wait to see him."

She clicked on the email and read:

Dear Attorney Amanda Harris,

It has come to our attention that you have violated the state-mandated rules that ensure all attorneys in the State of Massachusetts uphold their commitment to law and morality above all things.

We have decided to suspend your license to practice law for the time being. This is subject to reassessment after a period of twelve months.

Regards,

Massachusetts Board of Bar Overseers

Amanda gasped and dropped her phone just as another contraction swelled over her belly and across her lower back. The agony and confusion created a perfect storm. When the contraction subsided, she burst into tears and scrunched her face.

"Honey! It's okay!" Susan cried. She wrapped her arms around Amanda and cradled her hair. "I know you're scared, but you're healthy. The baby's healthy. And everyone you love is right here."

All Amanda could think about right now was the tremendous amount of energy, time, and worry she'd spent on the law. She'd worked tirelessly through undergrad to follow in her parents' footsteps. The admittance to Rutgers Law School had fit securely within the story she was telling herself, one in which her ex-fiancé and Amanda got married, had babies, and worked as a criminal justice lawyer in Newark.

Last year, she'd begun taking her own clients. Everything had gone smoothly. Almost everything.

"It's not that," Amanda gasped. "I mean, it is. I'm terrified of labor and delivery and all the pain that's coming. Don't get me wrong." She dried her face with the bedsheet. Was she too embarrassed to show Susan the email? Was it proof Amanda wasn't good enough to work at her mother's law firm?

"Just look," Amanda said, handing her mother the phone.

Susan read the email. Her face echoed confusion, then surprise, then shock, then anger. She glowered.

"It's that kid, isn't it?" Susan spat.

Amanda filled her lungs and held her breath. She felt another contraction around the corner and gripped the bedsheets to brace herself.

"His parents," Susan said. "Those uber-rich, old-moneyed Nantucketers. They were always so keen to brag that they knew the governor. That he came over for dinner sometimes." Susan's face was blood red. She burst to her feet, still clutching Amanda's phone. "They can't get away with this," she said. "They are entirely outside the law, asking the governor to pull strings like this. They're playing this like mobsters."

Sam returned with a cup of coffee and a bag of croissants. Sensing the shift in mood, he stalled in the doorway and blinked at Susan, then Amanda with confusion. A contraction wrapped around Amanda's back and made her feel genuinely possessed by a demon for the span of it. She felt the baby clambering for light. She wanted to tell the baby, *"Not now. I have so much to deal with."*

"What did I miss?" Sam asked after the contraction faded.

"Nothing," Amanda said, not wanting to get into it. "Mom's just trying to distract me."

Susan looked grim. Her chin quivered.

Amanda had read numerous books written by and for working mothers about how to juggle their professional careers with motherhood. How to ensure you don't get left behind in the workforce when you have a baby. How to maintain emotional connections with your children when you can't always be there. "Women can have it all in 2024," an essay said, "but just not everything at the same time. It takes balance. Organization." And that was something Amanda knew about herself. Generally, she was organized and didn't make mistakes.

But this situation was much bigger than her. And she had no idea if her career would survive.

Chapter Two

Wes Sheridan was back in his element. Dressed in a suit jacket and a button-down with a pair of corduroy pants, he manned the front desk of the Sunrise Cove Inn, greeting guests, giving advice, and smiling till his cheeks hurt. It wasn't often that Sam asked him to take over. But today was different. Today, Wes would have a brand-new great-grandbaby.

Wes wasn't afraid to announce that to anyone who cared to listen. "My granddaughter is at the hospital right now," he sang. "They're going to text me as soon as it happens. But you know how these things go. It could be tomorrow till the baby's here."

One of the guests, Frank Halibut, had been coming to the Sunrise Cove Inn nearly every April since Wes could remember. Anna used to call him "Frank Fish," which made Frank wallop with laughter. These were the memories of Anna that Wes liked the most. The silly, innocuous ones. The ones that reminded him why he'd fallen in love with her in the first place before everything had crumbled.

Frank came downstairs around four to rap his knuckles on the counter and say hello.

"There he is! Frank Fish," Wes said. "How is your trip so far?"

"You know I can't get enough of this place," Frank said. "It's heaven on earth."

"I always tell you the same thing. Move here. You'd be welcome."

Frank blushed. Like Wes, he'd lost his wife many years ago. Also, like Wes, he had a tremendously large family back in Providence, grandchildren and great-grandchildren he doted on. He couldn't leave them for good.

But instead of no, Frank just said, "Maybe one of these days."

From downstairs came the sound of the motor. It was sharp in Wes's ear, and he winced.

"What's all that racket?" Frank asked.

Wes laughed. "I told you my granddaughter's husband took over the inn, right?"

"Is that him downstairs? Is he digging to China?"

"He hired a construction firm to build a swanky new spa downstairs," Wes said. "They just started but aim to complete everything before the height of tourist season. I don't know the first thing about building a spa, but that sounds quick to me."

"They've got all this new technology now," Frank said with a wave of his hand. "But I'll tell you, Wes. I have no use for a spa."

Wes leaned toward him and stage-whispered, "Don't

worry. Even if the price goes up for everyone else, it won't for you. You're a part of the Sunrise Cove family."

Frank smiled in a way that allowed you to see how he'd looked as a younger man—filled with light and his entire life ahead of him. It was like a blink's worth of time travel.

"Tell me," Frank said. "Did your new manager ask your permission to build that spa downstairs?"

Frank was curious about how much power Wes had over the Sunrise Cove these days.

"He did," Wes said. At least, he was pretty sure Sam had. He needed to check his ledgers—in which he wrote down everything that happened to him as a way to stall his dementia—to be sure. "I told him it was a great idea." He continued to lie. "Inspired. I'm an old man these days. What do I know about the next wave of the tourist industry?"

"If you're old, I'm ancient," Frank joked. He was probably two years older than Wes, but his faculties remained intact. Wes sometimes struggled with his envy that other people were allowed all of their memories.

"I almost forgot to ask," Wes said. "Did you get my invitation?"

"I did," Frank said. "You're getting married again!"

Wes felt like a lit-up Christmas tree every time he thought about it. "Not long now! My niece Charlotte is planning every minute detail. You wouldn't believe it. Beatrice and I must have tasted seventeen different cakes."

"That's the kind of planning I could get behind," Frank said. "Consider this my RSVP."

Wes laughed. "I'll pass it along to the organizers. They told me I just have to put on a suit and show up. I'll be the guy at the front." Before he forgot, Wes scribbled in his notebook: *FRANK - YES - WEDDING*. That kind of fact would go right out of his head.

Frank belly laughed as, downstairs, the motor rang and roared. It sounded like a drill of some kind. Sam had said something about knocking down the basement wall and digging from the side to create an underground oasis. It had been miraculous to the builders that nothing plumbing-related was in the earth on that end of the inn.

Frank stepped out for an afternoon walk with a promise to eat dinner with Wes that night at the Sunrise Cove Bistro. Wes's son-in-law, Zach, was one of the best chefs on the island. It was a struggle for Wes to resist his buttery salmon, his thick and creamy mashed potatoes, and his Mediterranean-inspired dishes heavy with garlic. Zach and Christine's love blossomed after years of thinking of one another as enemies. They'd fallen for each other in that very kitchen. It was fit for a romance novel.

The motor cut out downstairs. Wes assumed the construction crew had finished for the day. It was nearly five, and he hadn't heard much of anything from the hospital crew in a few hours. He thrummed with a mix of fear and excitement.

A construction worker appeared at the top of the basement stairs and removed his hard hat. His face was coated in dust, and his eyes stirred with questions. He was looking at Wes as though he expected something from him. Had Wes forgotten something? Was he supposed to help somehow? Letting people down without knowing was one of the worst parts of dementia.

"Mr. Sheridan?" the construction worker began. "Do you have time to take a look at something downstairs?"

Wes brightened. He hadn't done anything wrong!

"Sure," Wes said. "Let's go." He propped up a sign on the front desk that said, "Be Right Back!" then followed the worker down the rickety staircase to the basement. Sam had said something about re-doing these stairs, too, hadn't he? Spa people wouldn't stand for it. The Google reviews would destroy them.

Downstairs was clearly a construction zone. There was dust and rubble everywhere. A few construction workers stood around in big blue jumpsuits and put their hands on their hips. One of them was on the phone, saying, "That's what I said, Roger. We can't go on."

The construction worker who'd led Wes downstairs had a name tag that read Conor. He brought Wes up to the cinder-block wall, where the team had drilled a hole approximately four feet wide by four feet tall. On the other side of the wall were very old wooden slats, green with moss and mold. It looked like the wall of a log cabin. Wes put his hand on the ancient wood and inhaled the smell of earth and age.

"We don't know what it is yet," the construction worker explained. "But we're worried about it."

Wes twisted to gape at him. "Worried?" None of this made any sense to him. He'd basically been raised in the Sunrise Cove. He'd worked here nearly every day of his life. It felt impossible there was something about the inn he'd never known about.

"Listen," the worker said, then knocked on the wood with his knuckles. There was a hollow sound, proof of air beyond the wall. "We think there's a room back there."

Wes stared at him. His blood pressure spiked. Was he dreaming? There were too many strange factors at play. Frank Fish was here. Amanda was having a baby. Wes was getting married. There was a secret room downstairs. Maybe none of it was real.

"Massachusetts is chock-full of historical sites," the construction worker said. He talked as though this sort of thing happened to him daily. "We're taught to immediately stop working and call in a historian so as not to damage anything. We have to preserve what's left behind, you know?"

Wes felt himself smile. He dropped his shoulders and studied the wall, behind which was a tremendous secret. He was nearly seventy-three years old. He hadn't assumed he could still be surprised.

"How about that?" he said finally, then laughed. The construction workers joined in behind him, cackling together beneath the earth. There was so much they didn't understand about the past or the future. But one thing was clear—everyone loved a mystery. They were on the brink of something enormous. Something life-altering. Something much better than a silly spa.

Chapter Three

From the Diary of Martha Smith
November 16, 1863

Nothing prepares you for walking all night in the frigid north. Thousands of stars spackle the night sky, and I crave their heat. I imagine them dropping out of the sky to warm me. My belly is big and pregnant and heavier every day. Everything I eat goes to it. The rest of me is skin and bones—tender sticks.

The most difficult part of the journey, besides the baby and the fear and the darkness, is the trust you have to have for the ones who guide you. It is not as though we come from a world where we learned how to trust.

Tonight, we took a boat across a frothing ocean. It was my first time on the water like that, and I wept quietly throughout the entire trip. I do not know how to swim. Neither does Virgil nor my sister Jane. If we tipped over, we were doomed. By the grace of God, we made it. And now we are here.

From a distance, the house looks massive—three stories along the water with a wraparound porch. A single lantern hung near the door, beaming its orange warmth. This is always our indicator. Here is someplace safe. As we neared it, the worst pain I've ever felt shot through my lower belly and across my back, and I fell to my knees. The pain left as quickly as it came. When I regained consciousness, I found Jane and Virgil on either side of me. Their eyes were wide with concern. They were worried about me but also about getting to the house before the sun rose.

It occurred to me that I'd wanted to flee because of the baby. But because of the baby, I might not make it all the way to Canada. To freedom.

Virgil half carried me to the door, where we were immediately ushered inside and brought downstairs. Everything was frantic. Another spasm of pain crept toward me. I could feel it, so I didn't focus too hard on the faces or whispered names. It was always this way when we were received. We were taken in and shoved in a room somewhere so that if someone had followed, they wouldn't be able to find us. This particular room is hidden behind a thick wooden wall that has a sort of trapdoor that allows entry and exit. I assume you can't really see it from the outside. I hope you can't.

That's what I mean about trust. You have to trust that people have arranged a safe house for you. That it's safe enough. But nothing is ever safe on the road.

Virgil doesn't want to believe I'm fully in labor. I write this between contractions. When the pain comes, I put a rag in my mouth and heave through the pain. I cannot make a sound. If we're too loud, there's a risk the people upstairs will throw us out. They can't risk it. There's no telling who's followed us from the South or what kind of demons have come to drag us back home.

I know I'll need help soon. I know the baby will scream and cry and put is all in danger. But I can't help but feel a strange shimmer of hope. My baby will be born in a free world. My baby will not be a slave.

Chapter Four

Present Day

A few hours after Amanda's career crumbled, she had to get serious about the next phase of her life. Squeezing Sam's hand with her left and Susan's with her right, she scrunched her face and pushed with all her might until her baby appeared. At the sound of the first cry, Amanda spasmed with relief.

"It's a girl!" the nurse announced.

Susan cried quietly and kissed Amanda on the cheek. "You did so good, honey."

Amanda laughed and opened her arms for her daughter. She was the tiniest thing she'd ever seen with jet-black hair and pink skin and fingers like flower petals. This had been the source of her ten months of acid reflux and vomiting and sleepless nights. As a swell of love came over her, she thought, *it was worth it. It was all worth it.*

Susan left Mom and Dad to enjoy their first moments with their baby alone. For the time being, Amanda forgot all about her suspended legal license. She kissed Sam, kissed her baby's toes. She mumbled about how exhausted she was and burst into laughter that made her cry again.

"You look so beautiful right now," Sam said, then snapped a photograph and showed it to her. She looked tired and slightly sweaty and happier than she'd ever been.

Another version of Amanda might have demanded Sam delete it. She might have quickly done her makeup and asked for another. But Amanda was a mom now. She wanted to live in the moment of this first impossible love.

"I thought you were going to faint," Amanda teased Sam after the initial shock fell away. "You were really pale."

"I'm not as strong as you. That's obvious," Sam said.

"I think she's probably having the weirdest day of all of us," Amanda said of her daughter.

"Poor little baby," Sam agreed. "We'll protect you. We'll make you comfy and safe."

Amanda's heart swelled. "Do you have that list handy?"

"The name list?"

"The dreaded name list." Amanda laughed. They'd bickered playfully about baby names for the duration of the pregnancy. Amanda wanted something classic like Sarah or Katherine or Annabelle, while Sam wanted something a bit more modern and unique.

"We've deleted almost everything on it," Sam said, bringing up the list on his phone.

"What's left?"

"Just one," Sam said. "Genevieve."

"Oh!" Amanda remembered now. Genevieve was her

pick. The name was taken from the patron saint of Paris from the fifth century. It meant "fair one."

"It's a big name for such a little girl," Sam said.

"She'll grow into it."

"I hope I can spell it," Sam joked.

Genevieve, the baby girl, let out a coo and wrapped her hand around one of Amanda's fingers.

"Welcome to the world, Genevieve," Sam said. "It's better with you in it."

Chapter Five

Grandpa Wes came to the hospital the following morning to meet Genevieve. His cheeks were shiny red apples as he held her and whispered sweet things. Amanda sat on the hospital bed, still feeling as though she'd been torn up and stitched back together again, but she smiled in a way that hurt her face.

"She's perfect, Amanda," Grandpa said as he handed her back gently. "Congratulations."

Grandpa Wes looked hesitant. He laced his fingers together and set his hands on his stomach. Sam arched his brow as the silence filled the room.

"I have some news," Grandpa Wes said.

Just then, the hospital door opened with more Sheridans. Christine and Lola had gone for coffee; Audrey had a big bag of bagels and another of cream cheeses. Beatrice waved from the waiting room behind them; she'd wanted to give Grandpa Wes space to meet his great-granddaughter alone. Amanda waved her in, too.

"What a crew!" Lola cried as she sat in one of the plastic chairs by the wall.

"Genevieve already knows we travel in packs," Susan said, bringing up the rear and shutting the door behind her.

"She's already one of us," Lola agreed.

"Grandpa was about to tell us something," Amanda said.

Everyone turned to look at Grandpa Wes. Susan's eyes echoed fear. With Grandpa Wes's dementia diagnosis, it was never far from anyone's mind that his health could turn on a dime. Amanda had spent too much time praying and hoping that he would make it through his wedding and a few happy years of marriage before everything fell apart. She hated thinking about this. But it always crept back into her mind.

Grandpa Wes smiled and cleared his throat. "Now that I have an audience," he began, "I can share something incredible. Something that affects all of us. Maybe you know that our genius manager Sam decided to break ground to build a basement spa for the Sunrise Cove. The construction workers started work this week. Not long after they began, one of them came upstairs to tell me they had something to show me. It was a reason they couldn't go on."

Sam's face was pale. "What happened? Is there more plumbing than we thought?"

Amanda could see him making calculations, wondering if he'd just made a grave error that affected Sunrise Cove's profit margins. He was always talking about profit margins. She loved that he cared about the Sunrise Cove Inn far more than a typical manager cared for a typical inn. He was a part of the Sheridan family now. He'd stitched himself into the history of the place.

"Not exactly," Wes said. "It seems they think there's a

hidden room downstairs. Something very historical in any case. They plan to contact a historian on our behalf who will investigate."

"What?" Lola cried. "A hidden room?"

"For what?" Susan demanded.

Wes raised his shoulders. "They didn't rip down the wall, so we couldn't see what was beyond it. But it's certainly fascinating, isn't it? I can't stop thinking about it! For my entire life, secrets lurked downstairs, and I never knew. And as far as I know, my parents had no idea either."

Everyone spoke at once with theories and questions. Because she was a newborn and exhausted with the world already, Genevieve slept through the mayhem.

Amanda waved her hand in the air. "Didn't you always say that your grandparents built the Sunrise Cove?"

"They did," Wes affirmed. "But the Sheridans lived on that land for generations before that. Remember that we're islanders deep in our blood. I remember my grandmother telling me about a terrible fire that almost destroyed the house where the Sunrise Cove Inn is today. It's possible they built over the secret room without really knowing what they were leaving behind."

This left everyone in the room speechless. The textures of time stood between them and the truth.

"I took several classes in law school about the legalities of historical sites," Amanda said.

Wes brightened. "We'll need your help every step of the way."

Amanda smiled. To most of her family, she remained a lawyer, even if she no longer had a license to practice. The memory of that thudded darkly in her stomach. But she didn't have time to deal with that now. There were secret rooms to explore. There was a baby to take care of. There was a wound between her legs that she needed to heal.

After Wes and Beatrice went home, Sam stepped outside to call the construction firm he'd hired to get more information about what they'd discovered and the next steps. Wes had said they worked with historians frequently.

This left Amanda and Genevieve alone with the Sheridan women: Audrey, Susan, Lola, and Christine. Mia was with Zach, and Max was with Noah, and both Audrey and Christine doted on Genevieve in the style of women who ached with recent memories of their babies.

"Before you know it, she'll be putting everything she can find in her mouth," Audrey warned.

"Enjoy every second of baby snuggles," Christine said.

"It'll be gone before you know it," Lola agreed with a brief glance at Audrey, the only baby she'd ever had.

Amanda was struck with a sudden image of herself twenty-five years from now awaiting the birth of her grandchildren, holding Genevieve's hand. She shook it out, smiled, and took Genevieve back in her arms, suddenly frightened of how quickly time could slip away.

Chapter Six

Wes and Beatrice returned home from the hospital and sat on the back porch with a pitcher of iced tea and their books. Beatrice was heavily into mysteries set in island locations like the Florida Keys or Orcas Island, and Wes liked to pretend to be a Sherlock Holmes's type and speak in an English accent to say, "Elementary, my dear Watson!" Beatrice had told him several times that the mysteries she read were nothing like Sherlock Holmes, but he didn't care. It made her laugh every time.

But they were too distracted to read this afternoon. Wes's head was filled with questions about the secret room, and he scanned through his available memories for some clue from his grandmother. She'd died so long ago, and there was so much Wes didn't know about her. As far as he knew, she'd kept no diaries. She'd been born in the early 1890s, had married his grandfather, had been instrumental in the building of the Sunrise Cove Inn after the fire, had had four children, and had died at the healthy age of eighty-two. She'd baked the very best chocolate chip cookies and played the flute. But what else did Wes really know about her? He'd been such a foolish boy. He should have asked her more questions.

"What are you thinking about?" Beatrice asked.

"What a foolish boy I was."

Beatrice laughed and laced her fingers through his over the tabletop. "All boys are foolish."

"No doubt."

"What do you really think is behind that wall down-stairs?" Beatrice asked.

Wes raised his shoulders. "It could be storage from the house that was there before the fire. Maybe I'll learn more about my great-grandparents or the ones before them. But I keep trying to mentally prepare myself for it to be a whole lot of nothing. Maybe it used to have some-thing that's since been destroyed by time."

Beatrice removed her reading glasses and studied him tenderly. "Or maybe it will be something incredible."

One of the last cardinals of the year landed on a tree branch near the porch. Wes perked up and nodded so that Beatrice could see its sleek red coat before it flew away. They'd initially bonded over their love of birds, and they went birding all the time, engaging in the mysticisms of the natural world. Sometimes Wes still went with Kellan, Susan's stepson. But Kellan attended college these days and didn't have much time.

Wes opened his ledger to recount what had happened at the hospital today. To do this, he would probably have to look up how to spell Genevieve's name again.

When he opened it, he saw the words: FRANK - YES - WEDDING.

"Oh! Frank Fish says he can come to the wedding," Wes said.

Beatrice smiled. "I wondered about him. Did you get his RSVP?"

"He told me himself."

Beatrice removed her phone and marked Frank as "yes" on the wedding app Charlotte had shown her how to use. Wes hated new-fangled technology, but Beatrice tended to welcome it. It was proof of her well-oiled brain working just fine compared to his.

"I showed you the plates Charlotte and I picked out, didn't I?" Beatrice flipped her phone around to show off beautiful floral china and silverware with ornate details along the edges.

Wes took the phone and paid special attention to why Beatrice liked these particular plates; why they mattered. He'd been alone for too long not to understand that you had to care about what people you loved cared about. It was part of being in love.

"I'm sorry if I talk about it too much," Beatrice said. "I'm just a blushing bride."

"You're a gorgeous bride. And you can talk about it as much as you want."

"How did I get so lucky?"

Wes and Beatrice went to bed around nine thirty every night. Sometimes Wes struggled to get to sleep immediately, but he always stayed still and stared through the darkness so as not to wake Beatrice. Gusts of wind flattened against the house and shook the window-panes. He did his best to let go and fade into sleep. He flattened his palms across the mattress and breathed slowly.

But all at once, he was in the middle of a nightmare.

Violent images came to him, and terror ripped through his heart. He only woke up because he was painfully, horribly cold, and wet. That, and someone was shaking him by his shoulders.

"Wes! Wes!" An old woman held his shoulders. Winds smashed against his chest and through his hair as rain splattered his shirt. He was barefoot in the sand at the edge of a violent ocean. It could only be the sound.

And then Wes realized this wasn't any old woman. This was his grandmother. She was here.

"Wes!" his grandmother cried. "Wake up! Come back inside!"

Wes blinked. "What are you doing here?" he croaked.

"Wes, you're sleepwalking," his grandmother said. "Come back in with me. We have to get you out of these wet clothes."

Wes shuddered from the chill. He realized he was only steps away from the frothing waves. It was like the ocean was hungry for him and wanted to swallow him whole.

As his consciousness returned, he realized that the old woman wasn't his grandmother at all.

"Beatrice?" Wes rasped.

Beatrice threw her arms around him and cradled him. She was crying but trying not to show it. Wes's shame crashed into him. He held her gently, then took her hand and led her inside rather than the other way around.

"What happened?" Wes asked once they were in the foyer.

"You got up and walked into the hallway. I was awake and followed you, thinking you were getting a cup of tea or something. But you just walked outside. I realized you were asleep and wanted to gently guide you back to bed. But you just kept going toward the water. I panicked and shook you awake." Beatrice tugged at her wet hair. "I know you're not supposed to wake up sleepwalkers. But the water was right there, and I was just so scared."

Wes ached with guilt. He slowly removed his wet pajamas and underwear and got in the shower. Beatrice remained close to him, waiting her turn. The way she looked at him terrified him. It was like she was waiting for him to have a complete mental break.

Wes had been doing so well lately. The ledger had worked for him. He'd hardly forgotten anything. He'd hardly been confused.

But wandering out into the night was the stuff of madmen.

When they were finally back in bed, Wes whispered into the darkness, "I'm sorry."

Beatrice took his hand under the sheets and squeezed it. "You're safe now. I won't let you get anywhere too far."

But Wes was too terrified to fall back asleep. Beatrice hadn't been Beatrice in his waking nightmare. She'd been his grandmother. It had been clear as anything in his mind's eye. Whatever had brought that on couldn't be trusted.

Chapter Seven

From the Diary of Martha Smith
November 25, 1863

This is my first entry since everything happened. Since my baby came into the world and brought with her tremendous pain that made me hallucinate what it must be like in hell. She came into the world quiet and reserved as though she already knew the cruelty lurking above this basement's surface. But almost as soon as she was with us, I was not. I was sick with fever, murmuring nonsense to Virgil and Jane as they tried to tend to me and the baby without alerting anyone of our troubles.

It was only when Virgil broke down and told Mr. Sheridan how ill I was that things started to get better. I have to guess I might have died had he not confessed.

Every day, Mrs. Sheridan brings medicine, foods with herbs, and tea. In the dark shadows of the basement, she holds my baby and dotes on her as Jane, Virgil, and I get *some much-needed rest. There is a kindness in Mrs. Sheridan's eyes that I hardly recognize.*

We've been here for nearly ten days. It's far longer than we've ever stayed anywhere since we left Georgia. I keep expecting Mr. and Mrs. Sheridan to tell us it's too dangerous; to throw us and the baby into the snow. The baby and I won't survive out there. Maybe Jane and Virgil will. But even that idea makes my blood boil: my sister and my husband allowed a second chance together while me and the baby died. I have to fight. Maybe I will beg the Sheridans to keep us till spring. It's unlikely to happen. But I am at their mercy.

November 26, 1963

Now that I am getting better, the days feel endless.

Since our escape, we've always had a sense of movement, of fear. And although it's been wretched and terrifying, we haven't been forced to sit with the reality of what we've done or where we're going until now. Everything we've ever known is behind us. And there's no way to know if we'll reach Canada safely.

To distract ourselves, I've begun teaching Jane and Virgil how to read and write. The Sheridans have four children upstairs and plenty of books for beginner readers. Jane has been jealous of my ability to read and write for years. Before I got pregnant, I worked in the big house for the lady of the house and her teenage daughter, who took pleasure in reading and writing and decided to teach me. I was embarrassed about this. Having preferential treatment was a lovely thing in many ways. But it made me feel like a house pet. And it made the people who worked the fields jealous and hate me.

But teaching Jane and Virgil is not as easy as I imagined it. Jane grows irate and gives up quickly. I think she wants to say horrible things to me but always looks at the baby and thinks better of it.

My baby will grow up learning to read and write. What a joy that will be.

November 29, 1863

Late last night, we planned to leave the Sheridans. There was a warm spell, a surprise this late and this far north, and Virgil decided we needed to make a leap to the next safe house. It was our never-ending journey toward Canada.

Mrs. Sheridan had let it slip that there were people from the South on the island looking for people like us. Her voice wavered. She was terrified for her family. People can only do the right thing until they destroy themselves doing it.

Mr. Sheridan arranged everything. A boat would be waiting for us at one in the morning on a beach a half-mile south of here.

But when Mr. Sheridan came to let us out of the basement room, he found me in a heap. My darling baby was as hot as flames. She'd gotten my illness. And her little body could hardly take it.

"You're not going anywhere," Mr. Sheridan said. He glanced at Virgil and Jane and set his jaw. A question hovered in the air between them.

I decided to answer for them. "You go," I said.

Virgil and Jane gaped at me. Jane touched my hair.

"We can't leave you and the baby," Jane said.

"You can. Virgil is right. You need to get farther north."

"We'll send word about where we are," Jane assured me after a strange pause. "You and the baby will be able to find us. It won't be forever."

I wanted to ask her how. But I also knew she was lying, both to me and herself, to make this easier.

Virgil, the only man I've ever loved, gave me a look that made my soul leave my body. It's impossible to know the future. But I truly felt, at that moment, that I would never see him again.

Maybe he was too embarrassed to kiss me goodbye.

I watched Jane and Virgil slip out of the basement room and heard their feet creak up the stairs. I felt them leave the house and me behind. I wept quietly until Mrs. Sheridan came downstairs with supplies for the baby's fever. We stayed up with her all night, doing whatever we could to calm her down and help her sleep. Mrs. Sheridan's face was strained. I knew it was unlikely my baby would make it through the night. And then, I would have stayed here on the island by myself for no reason. I would have given up my husband and my sister for nothing.

Early this morning, Mrs. Sheridan disappeared and returned with the island doctor. I was shocked when he walked through the basement door with his medical case and his round glasses. I couldn't believe Mrs. Sheridan had given herself up like this. But it was like she knew the baby would die without him.

He looked at me as though I were a ghost. Maybe I am. Perhaps we all are.

But he got right to work, tending to my baby as I watched on helplessly. I wondered if he was going to alert the people who'd come up from the South to trap us. Perhaps they'd arrest Mr. and Mrs. Sheridan. Maybe the children wouldn't have anywhere to go.

Everything was a risk. Time felt like a sharp knife.

Miracle of miracles, the doctor helped. The baby fell asleep and is still sleeping now. Upstairs, I can hear the footfalls of the children as they scamper and dance and play. I have no idea what they look like or what their names are. Their joy is such a strange contrast to my pain.

I am alone in this basement. Alone in the world, save for this baby. I pray she'll be all right.

Chapter Eight

Present Day

Amanda and Sam brought Genevieve home on a rainy morning in late April. Sam drove extra slow, almost dangerously beneath the speed limit, and muttered about other drivers on the road. "Be careful," he warned them. "I have a baby on board." Amanda was in the back seat next to the baby, smiling to herself. This was a scene of her life she'd always imagined: taking her baby home for the first time with the love of her life. It was better than she'd dreamed.

"This is your home, Genevieve," Sam announced as they pulled into the driveway. "I hope you like it. It's all we've got."

Amanda and Audrey had spent the winter decorating the nursery. They'd painted the walls a playful blue and stenciled sailboats and sea animals all over and painted them in pastel colors. A fluffy white rug covered the center of the hardwood floor with a rocking chair gifted from Susan. As Amanda placed Genevieve in her crib for the first time, she felt overwhelmed with the privilege of being able to raise a baby in such a remarkably beautiful and safe home.

A small part of her was jealous that Audrey and Noah had gotten the Sheridan House. But it was just up the road. She could go there whenever she wanted.

And Genevieve would think of it as a second home.

Amanda set up the baby monitor and padded downstairs to make lunch. Sam was at the kitchen island with his laptop, reading about historical sites in Massachusetts and the laws that protected them. Amanda knew he was excited about the prospect of the hidden room in more ways than one. Calling the Sunrise Cove Inn a historical site would draw even more tourism. He hoped that tourism boost would allow him the funds to build a complete spa in the back half of the property, which had been his original dream anyway. She kissed his ear. He was always on the hunt for the next best thing.

"The historian can't make it here for another two weeks," Sam said. "He insinuated that a big historical site was just discovered outside of Boston, and he's tied up."

"I wish he would have told you what it was!" Amanda removed cheese, cold cuts, lettuce, and onion from the fridge and began to prepare two massive sandwiches. Gone was salad-obsessed Amanda. She sometimes couldn't believe the extent of her hunger.

"It's good he needs time," Amanda said as she spread mayonnaise across a slice of wheat bread. "I won't be able to make it till then either. I want to settle in first with Genevieve."

Sam smiled. "That's right. You're our on-site legal counsel."

"That's me."

Amanda set down her knife and frowned. She realized she hadn't said anything to Sam about the email from the Massachusetts Board of Bar Overseers yet. It was one of the worst things that had ever happened to her. But it was dwarfed by so much goodness.

Amanda and Sam ate their sandwiches and recounted the craziness of the past forty-eight hours before Genevieve woke up and needed attention.

"It's only the beginning!" Amanda said with a laugh as she sped off.

It wasn't till the following day that Amanda returned her attention to her suspended law license. In the shadows of the nursery, she googled her ex-client Hilton Arnoult. At the sight of his face, a shiver went down her spine. She hadn't seen him since the day she'd lost the case and he'd been sent to prison.

Hilton Arnout looked made of money. His face was peaches and cream, his hair tousled and blond, his outfits Ralph Lauren and impeccable. He was Amanda's age or a little bit older, a Harvard graduate who'd only gotten in because his father golfed with the dean. She knew that because Hilton had told her; he'd practically bragged about it. He was one of those rich-blooded Americans who'd been given everything he wanted since birth.

When the Arnout family had reached out to the Law Offices of Harris & Harris last autumn, Susan had been over the moon. *"These people have real money, Amanda,"* she'd said after she took the first call. *"They want us to represent their son. Their precious son. It's going to be a windfall for us."*

Amanda tiptoed down the hall, clinging to the baby monitor with one hand and her phone with her other. Her mother answered on the fourth ring.

"Hi, honey!" Susan sounded busy and happy. Amanda pictured her at the kitchen counter with a bottle of wine and Scott by her side. "How are you and Genevieve?"

"We're wonderful," Amanda said, rubbing her chest.

"I know you said you wanted a bit of time to nest at home," Susan said, "but just let me know when I can come over. I can do anything. Cook. Clean. Hold her while you shower. Whatever."

Amanda smiled. "Thanks, Mom." She paused. "Listen, I wanted to ask you about the Arnout case."

Susan's tone shifted to business. "Those people have no right to do this to you. We need to take action immediately."

"How?" Amanda asked.

Susan was moving. Amanda could hear her footfalls through the phone.

"I mean, are you really sure they had something to do with it?" Amanda asked. "Maybe I made a mistake. Maybe the state board has me on something else."

"What? Amanda, no."

"Tell me, Mom. Did I mess up the Arnout case?" Amanda asked, her head throbbing. Suddenly, she desperately wanted to dive back through time and redo that case. To look at it from every angle again. To flip it over and turn it inside out. "I mean, would you have done it any differently?"

"If you remember, I worked with you on the Arnout case," Susan said. "You ran everything past me."

Amanda's heart thudded.

"The Arnouts refuse to admit that their perfect boy did anything wrong," Susan said, "and you're paying for it right now. But it won't be forever, okay? We're going to figure this out."

The baby monitor chirped and crackled. A second later came Genevieve's now familiar wails.

"I have to go," Amanda said.

"Good luck, honey. Don't think about the Arnouts too much. Remember, I love you. And this is a precious time."

"I love you, too."

Amanda hurried back down the hall to find Sam in the nursery. He sat in the rocking chair with their baby in his arms and rocked her gently back to sleep. Amanda took a moment to instill this image in her mind forever: her handsome husband with her adorable baby.

"Why don't you go rest?" Sam whispered. "I got it from here."

Amanda pressed her hand over her chest. "I'm going to lie down and relax."

Amanda made her way to her room. She lay down and listened to the thunderous quiet of the house.

But a moment later, she sat up, grabbed her phone, and searched online for an image of Hedwig and Clarice Arnout, Hilton's half-French, half-German father and French mother. Her heart pounded so much that she swore it would burst through her chest. The photograph showed them at a gala event for the governor of Massachusetts—no surprise there. Clarice was a beauty with a mean-spirited expression on her face and a waist she could probably fit her hands around. Hedwig was overweight but regal, like an English king from an older century. Amanda had met them several times as she'd prepared Hilton's case. They'd spoken to her very sweetly, their words like honey. They'd been so sure she was the one to get them out of "Hilton's silly situation." Were they really trying to destroy her career? She was only twenty-six years old! She'd just gotten started!

Maybe it was madness after childbirth or just the bravery that comes with being a mother, but Amanda wanted to handle this head-on, so she wrote an email to Hedwig.

Dear Hedwig Arnout,

I hope this email finds you well. The Massachusetts Board of Bar Overseers recently contacted me to announce that my license to practice law has been suspended. I am not the sort of person to make accusations, but I am the sort of lawyer to take responsibility for my actions. That said, if you have any specific queries regarding my work representing your son in his recent case, please let me know. May I remind you that I negotiated your son's prison sentence down from five years to one.

If it's all the same to you, I'd like my career back. I worked my entire life to build it.

Best,

Amanda Harris

Before she could stop herself, she sent it, then fell asleep. She came to with a start fifteen minutes later when she heard Sam knock on the door.

"Are you okay?"

Amanda sat upright. "I'm fine! I'm fine." But was she? A second later, reality thudded into her gut. She'd sent a horrible email to a very powerful man. She'd called his bluff.

"I was thinking about making popcorn," Sam said. "Would you like some?"

"Um?" Amanda's thoughts raced. She reached for her

phone, praying that the email hadn't actually sent. Perhaps it lingered in the Drafts folder and could be easily deleted.

But no. There it was in Sent.

Hedwig had already replied.

"Amanda? Popcorn?"

"Sure!" Amanda called. "Thank you." Her finger paused before clicking on the email. "She's asleep?"

"Sleeping like a baby," Sam joked.

"Ha. Ha." Amanda's smile erupted at the memory of her baby, fast asleep in that soft and pastel-painted nursery, but she bit her lower lip to tame herself. She had to deal with a professional emergency. For whatever reason, she'd decided to wrangle the beast from the comforts of her bath.

Perhaps the pregnancy and new mother hormones really had made her insane.

Dear Amanda,

So nice to hear from you. Thank you for this cordial message.

You know very well I wasn't pleased with your representation of my son. Just now, I sit with my wife one island away from yours and watch the sunset and imagine the horrors our boy is going through in that prison in Upstate New York. Nothing sways me from my belief that this is entirely your fault. Your mistake. And mistakes have consequences.

I know you are a trained lawyer. That you studied diligently and know the intricacies of the law. For this reason, I truly believe you can dig into that brilliant head of yours and come up with a solution that will work for all of us. You will craft a new defense strategy for my son. You will bring him home to me.

Cheers,
Hedwig Arnout

Chapter Nine

Wes booked an appointment with Dr. Hamilton for the end of the week. He didn't put the appointment on the calendar he shared with Beatrice in the kitchen because he didn't want her to worry. He wanted her to think of the sleepwalking incident as a one-time thing and not a symptom of a greater issue. But Wes was spooked.

Dr. Hamilton had been Wes's doctor for the better part of the past year. He specialized in memory care and had been genuinely surprised at Wes's progress since his diagnosis four years ago. When he'd learned of Wes's engagement, he'd clapped him on the back and said, "You son of a gun! You're beating all the odds."

But now, as Wes sat in Dr. Hamilton's office and told him about his recent nightmare, sleepwalking episode, and insistence that Beatrice was his grandmother, Dr. Hamilton's face grew pale. His tone was that of a typical doctor, preparing to give bad news.

"Nightmares are synonymous with worsening symptoms," Dr. Hamilton explained. "But I guess you already know that, and that's why you're here."

Wes swallowed and clutched his ledger. He'd brought it to ensure he didn't forget anything as he explained the incident to Dr. Hamilton. Now he wanted to throw it out the window.

"What should I do?" Wes asked.

"You're taking your meds? Getting enough sleep? Using your ledger?"

Wes nodded. "I'm doing everything." He was doing everything right!

"It's the nature of this disease," Dr. Hamilton said. "It's nobody's fault. It's just how things go."

Wes glowered at him. He suddenly empathized with the rage so many dementia patients usually demonstrated. It was horrendous to lose so much! To lose yourself!

"I want to ask you something," Wes said, forcing himself to look Dr. Hamilton in the eye.

"Anything."

Wes swallowed. "Do you think I should call off the wedding?"

Dr. Hamilton shook his head. "No, Wes. Absolutely not. The nightmare was a symptom, and maybe we're a few more notches down the road. But don't give up on something like that. It's probably been instrumental in keeping you well this long."

Wes was quiet. He thought of how beautiful Beatrice looked in the morning as she did the crossword at the kitchen table. All that light swam in off the sound.

"Listen," Dr. Hamilton said. "There's an experimental drug coming out soon. I'd have to do some tests to see if you're a candidate."

"What kind of experimental drug?" Wes immediately

thought of the seventies. He'd been in his twenties, and times had been very strange.

"It's a drug that helps clean the plaque off your brain cells," the doctor explained. "The plaque is what kick-starts the dementia in the first place."

"So all I've needed this whole time is a cleanup?"

Dr. Hamilton laughed. "It's not that simple. But it could slow the process down a great deal."

Wes knew enough not to get his hopes up. "What are the side effects?"

"Pretty typical so far. Weight changes. Poor sleep or too much sleep. Headaches. Dizziness. Confusion."

"I'm already pretty confused. That's the point."

Dr. Hamilton nodded. "We don't have to try it if you don't feel comfortable."

But Wes saw this as his only option. The other roads led to gray valleys and the darkness that came with the complete loss of his memory and soul.

"Let's do it," Wes said. He hoped he wasn't making a mistake.

Wes made his way to the Sunrise Cove that afternoon to meet with Frank Fish before returning to Providence. Frank was already seated on the back veranda with a novel splayed open in front of him and a glass of white wine. In his tweed suit, he looked like a professor of psychology. Wes didn't look half bad, either. He'd dressed in another suit jacket and a pair of dark jeans. He had to admit that Beatrice had elevated his style from "sloppy older man" to "sophisticated gentleman."

Frank stood to hug him, which felt like a surprise. It wasn't normal for older men to hug like this. It touched Wes's heart.

"Big rumors around the inn about that archaeological site downstairs," Frank said.

Wes chuckled. "We still don't know what's back there. The anticipation is killing me."

No, his mind corrected. *Your dementia is killing you.* He swallowed and turned as a server approached to take his order.

"Iced tea," he said, "and a salmon salad." Amanda said salmon helped with brain health.

"I'll have another glass of white," Frank said, "and a burger. No cheese."

"French fries?" the server asked.

Frank gave Wes a bug-eyed look. "Tell me you'll share?"

Wes's laughter bubbled up. Whether he lived another thirty years or died tomorrow, he couldn't resist french fries. "Okay."

The server retreated to the bistro kitchen to put in their order.

"Tell me," Wes said, "what are the rumors? What do the guests think we have downstairs?"

"I heard a little kid telling his mom there were mummies down there."

"Egyptian mummies?"

"I believe so," Frank said. "But another guy thinks it's all a scam to boost tourism. People don't like to believe in magical things anymore. Have you noticed that? Everyone is so cynical these days."

Wes tilted his head. "Usually, I see people during the best times of their lives. They're on vacation. They're celebrating their romantic love and their family love. They're swimming and sailing and eating and..." He trailed off. "What I mean is, I don't hear much cynicism. But that doesn't mean it's not out there."

"You live in a bubble," Frank said. "I should really move out here."

"You really should."

After lunch, Wes led Frank downstairs so he could see the wall. The concrete they'd torn apart before finding it was jagged and dangerous, and rubble was everywhere. Frank approached the wall slowly, then gave Wes a look. "Doesn't it make you think you're Indiana Jones?"

"You think the Holy Grail is back there?" Wes asked. He could get on board with everlasting life, he supposed. As long as he could spend it with the ones he loved on the most beautiful island in the world.

"Or the Ark of the Covenant," Frank said. He folded his lips. "Anna would have loved this."

Wes's chest heaved. He could practically see Anna in the basement with them now, folding laundry or searching for cleaning supplies or calling out, *"Wes? Can you come down here? I need your help!"* In his mind's eye, she'd been frozen forever in her late thirties.

"She'd be so proud of the life you built for yourself," Frank said, clapping Wes on the shoulder. "Anna loved squeezing all she could out of life."

"I never knew how she managed it."

Wes had a dark thought that Anna had "squeezed so much out of life" that she'd had an affair with Stan Ellis and drowned. But he promptly shook that away. He would always love Anna, warts and all. That was the nature of marrying someone. You were forced to see every single side of them; everything that made them unique— even the parts that didn't fit with you.

Chapter Ten

Genevieve was ten days old when she went to the Sheridan House for the first time. Amanda wrapped her up against her chest and walked her down the beach, listening for the first sounds of her family's laughter. Sam said he planned to meet her there after taking care of a few things at the Sunrise Cove, and dinner wasn't set till seven—three hours from now. But Amanda had a hunch that such a beautiful day meant most of the Sheridans would gather earlier to enjoy the sun. And when she turned to look up at the gorgeous house, she saw a heap of them across the porch—

Audrey, Max, Christine, Mia, Lola, Susan, Claire, Rita, and Steve. Steve was the odd man out, drinking a beer off to the side while the others listened with rapt attention as Rita recounted her recent case. She was a private investigator. It was how she and Steve met.

And now, they were finally giving their romance a real shot.

Earlier this year, Rita had been instrumental in bringing Claire's daughter back home after she disappeared. The story had exploded to reveal that Claire's longtime husband, Russel, was having an affair. He was now gone, and Claire was left to pick up the pieces of her life. "At least I'll always have the flower shop," she said so often it broke Amanda's heart.

Sometimes she wondered if Claire and Russel had truly been in love when they'd married. Maybe they'd been just the same as Amanda and Sam. Perhaps life had twisted up their love, contorting it into something they no longer recognized. Was there any way to avoid that heartache?

"There she is!" Audrey scampered down the porch with Max hot on her heels. "Come on, buddy." It was nearly May, and Audrey already had a sprinkling of freckles across her nose and upper arms. When she got closer, she picked Max up so he could see Genevieve up close.

"This is your cousin, Max," Audrey said. "You want to say hi?"

"Hi!" Max called a little too loud.

Audrey and Amanda chuckled.

"She's still just a little thing," Audrey breathed, placing her hand over Genevieve's head. "How do you stand it?"

"My heart breaks every day," Amanda said.

Up on the porch, Lola grabbed Amanda a chair and ordered her to sit.

"We're going to need more chairs," Susan said. "Dad and Beatrice are on their way."

"Andy and Beth, too," Steve said.

"What about Aunt Kerry? Uncle Trevor?" Christine asked. "Are they still in Florida?"

"They get back tomorrow," Steve said. "We're headed to Boston to pick them up."

"Can't believe they cheated on the island with all that tropical water," Lola said.

"Mom sent a picture of herself carrying a coconut filled with rum on the beach," Steve said with a laugh. "I think they're acting like teenagers."

"That's what can happen after your kids grow up." Lola caught Amanda's eye. "You stop worrying all the time and become a kid again."

"Amanda has never acted like a teenager," Audrey teased. She poked around a big bag of Doritos to select the ones with all three of their points.

"It's true." Susan giggled. "She vacuumed her room once a week. She did Jake's room, too."

Amanda rolled her eyes. "I was terrified of lice." She'd read in a science textbook that they could lurk anywhere —in your bed or your carpet or in her hair—and the idea had tormented her so much that she'd instigated a cleaning strategy that was borderline obsessive.

These days she was just clean in a normal way. Mostly.

Everyone wanted to take a turn holding Genevieve. A thickness went up her throat and threatened her breath as she watched so many others dote on her. She felt incomplete without her in her arms. It happened so quickly.

The screen door screamed open to bring Grandpa Wes and Beatrice. Amanda popped up and hugged her grandfather and filled her nose with his woodsy smell. She hugged Beatrice, too, but not as close. A small, childish part of her blamed Beatrice for taking Grandpa away from the Sheridan House. At her place was where he wanted to be now. But it still meant the end of an era.

Sam arrived a few minutes later with news. "I just got off the phone with the historian. He has time Wednesday afternoon to swing by the Sunrise Cove."

Everyone talked at once with excitement.

"I can't believe you haven't torn down the wall yourself," Lola suggested. "I'm dying of curiosity! What is back there?"

"Plenty of theories are circling the inn," Wes said with a laugh, then opened his ledger to read one. "A reporter came in to ask if it was true we had Mormon gold back there."

"Mormon gold?" Susan cackled. "People are so creative."

"Don't let anyone take our Mormon gold, Sam," Christine warned.

"Whatever it is, I'm hoping it'll make the inn a historical site," Sam said.

"The Sunrise Cove has been around so long that it should be called a historical site in and of itself," Christine declared.

"It hasn't been around as long as whatever's in that room," Sam said.

"I was sorry to hear the spa is off the cards," Beatrice said. She put a Tupperware container of banana bread on the big table, and the decadent smell swanned over them. "I was looking forward to some pampering after all this wedding chaos is through!"

"I'll send you to the Katama Bay Spa any time you want," Wes said, touching her hand.

Amanda and Audrey locked eyes for a split second. Both were thinking the same thing. Stan Ellis, the man who'd accidentally killed their grandmother, was engaged to the woman in charge of the Katama Wellness Spa.

Nancy Remington. The twisty past was never far from anyone's mind.

Audrey raised her shoulders and smiled as though to say, *what can you do? Life is strange.*

Dinner was served at seven. By that time, the rest of their crew had arrived: Andy, Beth, and their two children; Lola's husband, Tommy; Christine's husband, Zach; Susan's husband, Scott, and Audrey's boyfriend, Noah. Fire spat across the grill to cook shish kebabs and chicken burgers, and Amanda's mouth watered. When she filled her plate, she caught Audrey watching her with a big grin.

"It's the breastfeeding, isn't it?" Audrey teased. "I was starved for months."

"I can't get enough!" Amanda said.

With the baby fast asleep in the shadows of the living room, Amanda sat with her mother, Lola, and Audrey at the edge of the porch so that their legs swung over the side. The air was fresh and losing its heat, so Audrey threw a blanket over herself and Amanda to keep their legs warm. Amanda took a bite of the chicken burger, and her mouth oozed with mayonnaise and spicy sauce. She sighed and took another. Behind her, she could hear the comfortable rhythm of Sam's voice as he chatted to Wes about the logistics of meeting the historian this week. She was thrilled that Sam always ran everything by her grandfather and kept him in the loop. He didn't have to. But nobody wanted Wes Sheridan's link to the Sunrise Cove to falter. It was his blood.

Lola and Audrey spoke over one another excitedly about Lola's new magazine article and the pitches Audrey was sending to literary journals across the country. This left Susan and Amanda alone for the first time in a while.

Amanda remembered, with a jolt, that she needed to confess.

She set down her chicken burger. "I might have poked the bear."

Susan raised her eyebrows. "What does that mean?"

Amanda explained the hugely idiotic thing she'd done. She'd written to Hedwig Arnout.

"I don't know what I was thinking. Maybe that telling him I knew what he was up to would embarrass him so much that he'd make a phone call and get this mess out of my hair? But it only made matters worse."

Susan's face drained of color. Amanda could read her mind. She thought Amanda was naïve, and in many ways, she was. She was a brand-new lawyer up against elite Nantucketers with the governor on speed dial. Men like Hedwig could destroy her with the wave of his hand.

"Don't panic," Susan said quietly. She squeezed Amanda's shoulder. "Once you get settled in a bit more with Genevieve, we'll take action. But don't do anything without me."

"I won't," Amanda assured her.

Hubris had led her to write that email. Worse is that hubris had made Hedwig call the dogs on her career in the first place. Amanda needed to be tactical. She needed to step away from the situation, analyze the players and the stakes, and leap when the time was right. She wouldn't give up her career. Not because some rich playboy named Hilton Arnout thought he was beyond the law.

It was true that being a criminal justice lawyer was sometimes morally difficult. Susan and Amanda's father, Richard, had represented heinous criminals over the years. They'd been featured on the news, speaking about their clients' rights. During a murder case more than ten years ago, Amanda asked her mother, "Do you think he did it?"

Susan answered, "It doesn't matter if he did or didn't do it. It's up to me to ensure the law treats him just the same as it would anyone else. The verdict is up to the jury."

This had stuck with Amanda: the fact that criminals had rights. You couldn't just throw people under the bus based on cultural opinion.

But despite Amanda's tireless efforts and two appeals, Hilton Arnout had been sentenced to prison. The jury had sent him there. That had nothing to do with Amanda. She should have been able to wash her hands of it by now.

Late that night as she nursed Genevieve and laid her gently in her crib, Amanda thought about the weight of the world and how little Genevieve knew of it after ten days of life. She tried to imagine what it was like to be Mr. and Mrs. Arnout and face the consequences of their son's actions. They'd done everything to get him through the first twenty-seven years of his life with flying colors. Perhaps their anger came from a sense of failure. Of having hid Hilton from the chaos of the world, only to have him crash-land in prison. Somebody had to take the blame. And right now, it was Amanda.

Chapter Eleven

From the Diary of Martha Smith
December 11, 1883

Mrs. Sheridan caught me writing this morning. The look in her eyes said she didn't think any slaves could read or write. She had the good sense not to say so. She brought more supplies for the baby: medicine, clothes, blankets. The basement room has become nearly cozy despite the damp air. She also brought a delicacy for me: a Christmas biscuit. The recipe runs in the Sheridan family.

I asked her when she married Mr. Sheridan. She said she was eighteen years old. She had her first baby at nineteen, and all the others before the age of twenty-five. She said her body ran itself ragged. As we spoke, I accidentally showed the palm of my right hand, where the scar goes all the way across. She was pale. I knew she wanted to know what had happened, but I didn't want to tell her.

The baby is healthier and fatter every day. It's hard to believe we almost lost her. Mrs. Sheridan thinks I should *give her a name soon. I realized I've been so frightened for her life and for mine that I haven't considered it.*

A few ideas: Mary. Nadia. Esther, after my mother. Jane, after my sister.

I wonder how far Jane and Virgil have gotten. I wonder if they really will find a way to send word back. I wouldn't dare travel with a baby in the winter, but Mr. Sheridan says I can stay until spring or as long as I need.

December 14, 1883

Late last night, the basement door burst open. I woke up with a start, sure that they'd come for me. That I was being captured and dragged back to Georgia.

Two other ex-slaves walked into the basement room. One of them carried a twentysomething ex-slave whose leg was bandaged but bleeding through. He laid him on the bed that had once been Jane's as Mr. and Mrs. Sheridan hurried in to nurse his wound. I was too scared to ask what had happened. The injured young man shook violently and sweated all over the mattress. It didn't take long before he passed away. It was infected, Mrs. Sheridan said.

The young man was shot as they'd made a getaway to the boat that would take them to the island. Somehow they'd made it this far. But he'd been unlucky enough to die in my basement.

The morale was low. Mr. Sheridan took the body somewhere and left me here with the men the deceased had left behind. After a very long silence, one of them said they were from Virginia. They were brothers, or at least they all had the same mother. I recognized the weight of what they'd lost and cried with them.

After a time, they told me they planned to head farther north tomorrow. They wouldn't stop for anything. They invited me to go with them and said they would protect me and the baby. But I resisted. I feel a comfort in my little room beneath the earth. The baby and I are regaining our strength. And I still hold out hope that Jane and Virgil will contact me here when the time comes.

December 25, 1883

I was allowed upstairs for two minutes.

It's Christmas Day, and the Sheridans have celebrated accordingly. They decorated a big tree with tinsel and candles and cooked a big meal. I could smell the yams and turkey from the basement, and my mouth watered.

Mrs. Sheridan wanted to show me how her children had all fallen asleep by the roaring fire in front of the Christmas tree. She'd spent so much time with my baby, and it was time that I see hers. It was true they looked adorable, snuggled up together beneath blankets, overstuffed with turkey. Mrs. Sheridan gave me a big platter of food to take downstairs with me, and I ate it slowly, trying to save it as long as I could.

I decided to name my baby Mary, after Jesus's mother. It is truly because of him that I have found my way to these people. It is because of him that I am safe.

Chapter Twelve

Genevieve was two weeks old the day the historian came to Martha's Vineyard. Amanda was torn. All she wanted was to stand in the dank basement with Sam and Grandpa Wes and watch the wall fall between this world and the past. But it destroyed her to leave her baby behind for more than a second.

"It's going to be all right," Audrey assured her. They were in the foyer of the Sunrise Cove. Audrey had a sleeping Genevieve wrapped against her chest. She wore her easily, with a typical Audrey-laissez-faire attitude, and reminded Amanda that she'd only be in the basement an hour at the most. "I'll just be writing in the bistro," Audrey reminded her. "Come up whenever you're ready."

Audrey disappeared in the bistro to take her typical seat near the window. A server followed her, then ducked back around to make Audrey's tea and favorite grilled cheese. She was Sheridan royalty. Everyone always knew what she wanted.

Sam and Grandpa Wes chatted with the historian outside on the lawn. It was early May, a gorgeous sixty-five degrees, and Amanda wore a pair of flare jeans and a sweeping blouse. Her stomach was receding quicker than she'd anticipated, but she'd also bought a bigger pair of jeans just to feel comfortable. No use destroying her mental health over a pair of pants. (Looking back from a mother's perspective, she couldn't remember why she'd cared so much about being thin in the first place. There was so much else to think about.)

George Whitehead, the historian, had graduated from Harvard undergrad and had a masters from Cambridge and had been featured on The HISTORY Channel, in the Smithsonian, and at the Anthropology Museum in Mexico City. He wore a tweed suit and very small rectangular glasses that seemed to be more for aesthetics than use. He was maybe fifty years old.

"Dr. Whitehead, this is my granddaughter Amanda. She's the lawyer I was telling you about," Grandpa Wes introduced.

She shook his hand and was surprised at how warm and soft it was. "Pleasure to meet you. Thank you for coming so quickly. Sam said something about a newly discovered site by Boston?"

"It turned out to be a fluke if you can believe it," Dr. Whitehead said with a laugh. "People want to believe they've discovered history so bad that they concoct all kinds of lies to support their stories. I don't think they always know they're lying until they're in over their heads."

"Is that right?" Grandpa Wes put his hands on his hips.

"People will do all kinds of things for fame and glory,"

Dr. Whitehead said. "That's one thing we've learned over centuries of studying human behavior. Hubris is the fall of man."

There was that word again, Amanda thought. Hubris. During a game of Scrabble last night, she'd even managed to use it to get twenty-two points. She'd defeated Sam by five.

Dr. Whitehead cleaned his glasses with a paisley handkerchief. "It's always good to have a lawyer on your side," he said, giving Amanda a kind smile.

Amanda's stomach lurched. Nobody but Susan knew about her suspended license. She wanted to tell Sam; she really did. But between baby snuggles and feedings and talk of the "mysterious room" in the Sunrise Cove, news of Amanda's potential loss of career had slipped through the cracks. Was it a lie of omission? Or was it just Amanda's fear?

Grandpa Wes, Sam, Amanda, and Dr. Whitehead donned construction hats and proceeded to the basement to meet with the construction crew Sam had initially hired to build the spa. With Dr. Whitehead's guidance, they'd spent the better part of the morning ripping out the rest of the concrete wall that covered the wooden slats of the hidden one. Now that it was cleared, stones were piled in the corners, and even more dust coated the basement stairs. But the mossy wall was uncovered completely.

Dr. Whitehead paused in the middle of the basement and glared at the staircase. "Where is Bart? He said he was coming down here."

A split second later came a man's voice at the top of the steps. "I'm on my way! Had to swap out a lens."

Dr. Whitehead breathed a sigh of relief as a thirty-something man with bottleneck glasses burst down the stairs. Around his neck hung a strap attached to a sleek video camera. Amanda had read over the paperwork and, together with Sam and Grandpa Wes, had agreed it was appropriate to film the event. Sam wanted to use it for promotional material down the line. Wes had confessed he really wanted to be on television.

Bart set up in the corner of the room so that Dr. Whitehead was the central figure, and Amanda, Grandpa Wes, and Sam hovered behind him. Dr. Whitehead spoke to the camera as though he spoke to a massive studio audience and even added a hint of an English accent, presumably picked up from his years at Cambridge. Amanda smiled to herself. Everyone on television was a fake.

"My name is Dr. George Whitehead, and today, I find myself in a very exciting position," Dr. Whitehead began. "I stand in the basement of the historical Sunrise Cove Inn of Martha's Vineyard, where the owners have discovered what seems to be a secret room. Together, we are going to open the secret door between this room and the next and see what's inside."

Amanda's thoughts raced. She searched across the wooden slats for some sign of a door but came up with nothing. It was all green and brown and black. She flinched when she realized she should have worn a face mask to protect herself from spores. But before she could run upstairs, one of the construction workers passed out N95 face masks, and she slipped it over her mouth and nose. It was hard not to think of the pandemic and all the fear that had come with it.

But this was a moment of excitement. It was a historic occasion.

Dr. Whitehead continued to speak to the camera without a mask. He explained that "secret entrances" like this were quite common more than one hundred years ago. "There must be a spring somewhere," he explained as he rapped on different parts of the wooden wall. On the other side was a hollow echo. "You hear that?" he asked the camera. "The room on the other side is quite large. I would guess ten feet by ten feet? Not a mere closet. That's for sure." His voice shifted to a higher pitch. It was clear he was excited.

It took Dr. Whitehead some time to find the trapdoor. After a while, he switched to his normal talking voice and grew disgruntled. Bart kept filming, but his arms looked tense and tired. Amanda had begun to suspect that they would need a chainsaw to get through when—suddenly—came a soft pop, like the sound of a champagne bottle opening.

Dr. Whitehead returned to his vaguely English accent immediately. "Did you hear that?" His eyes were alert. Right in front of him, part of the wall had jumped from the rest of it to reveal a tiny latch. On the count of three, Dr. Whitehead pulled up the ledger and opened the door. The sound of the hinges creaking and groaning made it clear it hadn't been opened in decades, maybe centuries. Amanda held her breath.

Nobody was allowed inside the room yet except for Dr. Whitehead and Bart with the camera. Amanda held a flashlight inside from the doorway and traced the corners, the ceiling, and the floor. The ceiling was blackened in some places, presumably from the fire that had destroyed the house where the Sunrise Cove Inn now stood. There were two full beds, a bunk bed, a massive trunk that looked fit for buried treasure, a small bookshelf with dusty books on it, and a broken cabinet. In the farthest corner was what looked to be a baby's crib. Amanda's heart lurched. She stumbled back, imagining a baby in this room, so far beneath the earth. Why? What was it for?

Grandpa Wes couldn't stop shaking his head with awe. He wiped his brow with his kerchief and spoke through his mask. "I can't believe it. I must be dreaming."

Sam touched the small of Amanda's back and laughed with surprise. There was nothing to say. Not yet.

Amanda was getting claustrophobic. As Dr. Whitehead continued to monologue to the camera, she told her grandfather and husband she was headed upstairs. They followed after her wordlessly. When they emerged on the landing, the curious gazes of at least twenty pairs of eyes met them. Everyone spoke at once, demanding what they'd seen. Amanda accidentally broke the string of her mask as she pulled it off.

"What was down there?" A female guest with a black bob made fists, her eyes enormous.

"What did you find?" another guest badgered.

Sam removed his mask and put on his "manager" face. "I can't share details right now," he began, "but we've discovered something historical downstairs. A site that is yet to be fully understood."

Amanda felt strange and euphoric. As the guests threw more questions at Sam and Grandpa Wes, she weaved through the crowd and turned to corner to find Audrey and Genevieve. Genevieve was awake but happy, kicking her feet at Audrey, who was smiling down at her. It was a beautiful portrait.

* * *

It didn't take long for the guests at the Sunrise Cove to post about the event on social media. They felt a part of something spectacular and once in a lifetime, and they had to announce it to the world. Their excitement at seeing Dr. George Whitehead in the flesh was palpable, too. A few dared take photographs of him as he left the basement covered in dust. Others posted photos of the Sunrise Cove from the outside and said, "Mystery at the Sunrise Cove! We're dying to get in the basement to see what's down there. Tell us your secrets, Mr. Sheridan!"

Amanda watched the news unfold from home. Genevieve was asleep upstairs, and Amanda attempted a noodle recipe she knew Sam liked. Sam was on the couch with a glass of wine and the television on. He was weary but excited. When he flipped to the news, they were already talking about the Sunrise Cove.

Dr. Whitehead had sent the news a video of himself walking through the trapdoor of the basement, but nothing else. It was like a "teaser" video. The anchors speculated wildly about what could possibly be down there.

"It's another historic event in Massachusetts," one of the anchors finished happily. "We have a very old American history, and there's always something new to surprise us from the past."

Amanda took a seat on the sofa while the noodles boiled and watched Sam's face. He was rapt.

"We got so many reservations today," he explained. "For late summer, fall, and even winter. A few people asked if they could come next summer already. It's barely May 2024, and we're filling up for June 2025!" He rapped his fist against his thigh and smiled.

Amanda knew he took this seriously. He wanted the Sunrise Cove Inn to flourish. He wanted to prove himself.

Chapter Thirteen

Wes spent that evening watching the news with Beatrice. Twice, they showed a clip of him on television wearing his N95 and bracing himself as Dr. Whitehead entered the trapdoor. He'd been terrified that Dr. Whitehead was walking into something sinister; something that should never have been opened in the first place—like in that film *The Mummy*. But when he shone a flashlight through the ten-by-ten space, his heart had opened with awe. Whatever that room was, it had a story. And Dr. Whitehead was going to get to the bottom of it.

"You look so handsome," Beatrice said when they showed Wes on screen again. She stood behind him and swept her fingers through his hair, then lightly massaged his head. Wes could have swooned.

"What do you think it was?" Beatrice asked as they got ready for bed later that night.

Wes wasn't sure. "Dr. Whitehead said it's at least one hundred years old and that it was absolutely a part of the burnt-down house. He has theories about what it was used for. A hiding place of some kind." He stroked his five o'clock shadow and sat on the edge of the mattress. "He thinks it was covered up by accident when my grandparents built the Sunrise Cove."

"How will he put together the story of the past?" Beatrice asked as she lay back in bed, adjusting the pillow beneath her head.

"I assume he has his ways," Wes said with a laugh. "It's scary how much he's uncovered. He was at a Mayan site a few years back when he noticed a stone that looked a little out there, and he used it to find an enormous stone floor beneath the sand. It was completely preserved."

"He's like a magician. He can see through time," Beatrice said.

Wes wanted to make a joke about that. To suggest that Dr. Whitehead see through time to find the youthful and unimpaired version of Wes that still existed somewhere inside him.

Wes was still in the process of testing to see if he qualified for the brand-new drug Dr. Hamilton mentioned. When he was there, he couldn't read Dr. Hamilton's expressions enough to guess if he passed the tests or not. He wondered if not being able to read people as well was a part of his decline. He assumed so.

Perhaps because of the chaos at the Sunrise Cove, Wes was again plagued with nightmares. In them, he was a younger man still living at the Sheridan House with Anna. For some reason, he needed to talk to her and tell her something so desperately that it ate him up inside. But every time he entered a room to speak to her, she left through another exit, so he never saw anything more than the back of her head.

"I'm in here, Wes!" Anna called from every room.

He chased her until he staggered to a halt on the back porch, putting his hands on his thighs to steady himself. Anna wore a white dress and stood at the far edge of the dock. She faced the Vineyard Sound. The wind swept through her long, thick hair and her dress, and she raised her hand to wave to someone. Wes reached out. He wanted to tell her to get away from the water, that it would kill her, but when he opened his mouth, he couldn't speak.

Wes woke up with a gasp and pressed his hand to his chest. His pajamas were soaking wet with sweat. Bit by bit, the world came back to him. Beatrice was fast asleep, curved away from him. He was in the house they lived in together. Not the Sheridan House. Anna had been dead for nearly thirty years.

What had he wanted to ask Anna? What had he been so desperate to know?

Wes grabbed his ledger and tiptoed through the dark to sit at the kitchen table. He recorded everything he could of the nightmare. Maybe it would serve him someday. Perhaps he could share it with Dr. Hamilton, who would explain that the dream didn't mean Wes was getting sicker. *"All it means is you and your first wife have unfinished business,"* Dr. Hamilton might say. And Wes could respond, *"Tell me something I don't know!"* and laugh darkly.

* * *

Wes returned to the Sunrise Cove the following morning to meet Sam and Dr. Whitehead. Amanda had been up all night with the baby and couldn't make it, but she sent numerous text messages about how to handle the situation from a legal standpoint. Wes hoped Sam would remember them. They'd already flown out of his head.

Dr. Whitehead had friends with him—other historians who specialized in this specific arena of history.

"And what arena of history is that exactly?" Wes asked.

Dr. Whitehead's glasses glinted. He took a little too much time to speak, as though he wasn't sure he wanted to share. "The Civil War."

"That far back? Wow," Sam said.

"That's our assumption thus far," Dr. Whitehead said. "The van is stocked with specialty equipment that will allow us to handle and test various items that have been kept in the room for more than one hundred years. It's best not to bring anything into the light or out of that air. That environment is all those items have known."

That made sense to Wes, he guessed. But as Dr. Whitehead and his historian friends headed downstairs, he burned with more questions. This was his family history. He had to know more.

"You don't think it could have been part of the Underground Railroad, do you?" Sam muttered.

Wes's adrenaline spiked. He hadn't considered this. "Did the Railroad come this way?"

Sam removed his cell from his pocket and typed furiously. Wes would never maneuver his cell the way the younger generations did. His clumsy thumbs always hit the wrong buttons.

"Looks like it did," Sam said, showing Wes a cartoon map that illustrated one of the paths of the Underground Railroad.

"We don't know anything for sure yet," Sam continued to mutter to his phone as he searched for more information. "But this is intriguing. Crazy intriguing. I have to talk to Amanda. See what she thinks."

It certainly captivated Wes to consider that his family had been involved in the Underground Railroad. Everybody wanted to believe their families were good people; that they'd done the right thing in a historical context. Nobody sat well with themselves when their family had been slave owners or Nazis, even if it had nothing to do with them.

Wes tried to add up the years and figure out who had owned the property back in the 1860s. His grandfather had been born in the late 1880s; his grandfather's grandfather had been born in the 1830s or 1840s. Maybe he could ask Susan about their genealogy. She kept a good record.

Natalie worked the front desk that morning, waiting for Wes to relieve her of her duties. "The guests won't stop pestering me about what's downstairs," she said. "Like I look like someone who knows anything!"

Wes laughed and eyed the dark basement door. It looked like a cave.

"Did they say anything else this morning?" Natalie asked.

"They think it's from the Civil War period," Wes explained. He decided not to mention their speculation about the Underground Railroad. It excited him so much, and he didn't want to be wrong.

"But don't tell the guests it's Civil War-related yet!" Sam hollered from the office next to the front desk. From where Wes stood, he could see Sam looking over paperwork, his head bent. If Wes tricked his mind for a split second, he could imagine that was himself back there. That he had paperwork to tend to, and Anna was coming back soon with their young girls. He shook his head of the image.

"It's all fascinating," Natalie said. "How many times have I been in that basement?"

"Think about how I feel," Wes said. "I was practically raised here."

The morning continued the way it had since the big discovery downstairs. Guests paraded past him and peppered him with questions. They called him "Indiana Jones." They laughed with him about how "strange and fun" it all was. Wes felt boisterous and slightly manic. He sent guests all over the island for hikes and restaurant picks and beach walks, reminding them to put on sunscreen. "It's not that warm out there yet, but the sun can bite you anyway." He remembered his own girls' sunburns and how they'd wept with pain.

Frequently, he made notes in his ledger. Every once in a while, he caught himself thinking, *as soon as I get that new medication, I won't have to use this ledger anymore. I'll remember everything again.* It wasn't logical, maybe. But he loved thinking about it.

Sam came and went and came back again. He watched the baby in the afternoon so that Amanda could take a shower and have a nap, then hurried back to the Sunrise Cove to chat with Zach about the approaching dinner menu. Everything about the day felt smooth and glowing with expectation for whatever came next.

The news crew came out of nowhere.

Wes couldn't help but smile at Rhonda Evans as she entered the foyer. She was one of the news anchors who'd shown a video of the Sunrise Cove last night, and she wore a smart navy blazer and her hair in a sharp bob. She strode toward him with a confidence she must have trained herself to have. Or were some people born with that much confidence? Wes had never had it.

"Good afternoon! Welcome to the Sunrise Cove Inn," Wes greeted her.

Rhonda smiled. "Are you Wes Sheridan?"

"I am!" Wes was surprised she knew his name. A blush crawled up his chest. "And you're Rhonda Evans."

Rhonda laughed in a big and brassy way and waved for her camera guy to get the shot. "Do you mind if I interview you for a little special on Sunrise Cove tonight?"

"Not at all."

Wes had decided long ago that he wanted to be filmed as much as possible before his brain gave up on him. He wanted to be remembered. It was vain, but it was the truth.

Rhonda smiled, fixed her already perfect hair, and raised her microphone to her mouth. The cameraman said, "Action," and Wes smiled goofily. When he tried to stop, he smiled even more.

"Good evening. Welcome to the Sunrise Cove Inn on Martha's Vineyard. As we mentioned last night, a secret room has been discovered in the basement of the old inn that was, according to some reports, sealed off after the original building burned to the ground and the Sunrise Cove Inn was built in its place." She turned to look at Wes. "I'm here with Wes Sheridan, the longtime owner of the Sunrise Cove Inn. Wes, how long has your family owned this property?"

Wes's neck was slick with sweat. "Oh, hundreds of years," he said. "My father always told a story about his long-ago coming here from Ireland to whale professionally. My grandparents were the ones who built the

Sunrise Cove Inn back in the day. That was after the fire."

"And they didn't know anything about the secret room?"

Wes raised his shoulders. "They never mentioned it to me."

"Is it possible that they covered it up on purpose? To hide a secret?"

This hadn't occurred to Wes. "I don't see why they would have done that."

Rhonda's eyes flickered. It felt like she dug through his mind, searching for a potential story. Wes was having second thoughts about being on television.

"But it's possible, isn't it?" Rhonda said. "I'm sure your grandparents didn't tell you everything."

"I was a kid. Probably not," Wes said.

Rhonda smiled. "Can you tell us your plans at the Sunrise Cove now that the room has been discovered? Will there be a public reveal? Will you make the inn a historical site?"

Wes felt flustered when he realized this wasn't a question for him. It was for Sam. But as he pondered what to say so as not to look like a fool, the foyer door burst open again to bring in two balding men in suits. Wes couldn't forget that his main job right now was to operate the front desk. He put on a smile and said, "Good afternoon! Welcome to the Sunrise Cove Inn."

The men in suits didn't care that Rhonda was filming. They strode right into the shot and blocked her.

"Excuse me?" Rhonda cried as her cameraman turned off the camera.

"Are you the owner of the Sunrise Cove Inn?" the man on the left asked Wes. He removed something from a manila folder and licked his lips like a cat who'd just eaten a mouse.

"I am," Wes said, although the legalities of that were more complicated now.

The man put a document in front of him. Wes blinked at it but needed his reading glasses to see it clearly.

"We hereby state that the Sunrise Cove Inn is closed for the foreseeable future," the man said formally. "It is a historic site in the State of Massachusetts and requires a thorough analysis before reopening. If it ever reopens in the same capacity again."

Wes gaped at him. "What are you talking about?"

The man set his jaw. "It is up to us to uphold the historical nature of all Massachusetts sites."

"You don't understand." Wes pulled at his hair. He felt as flustered and confused as a very sick old man. "We need the inn. We've always needed the inn to survive."

But the men turned around without another glance and retreated from the foyer. Wes and Rhonda stared down at the legal document, and Rhonda had a hungry glint in her eyes. She looked at her cameraman and asked, "Did you get any of that?" When the guy said yes, she snapped her fingers. "Yes! Now that's a wild story."

Wes's heart thudded. He was in over his head.

Chapter Fourteen

Genevieve had just fallen asleep when Sam burst through the door. He was frantic, his eyes bloodshot, waving around a folder. Amanda pressed her finger to her lips to remind him to stay quiet. He couldn't wake the baby.

"I need your help," Sam rasped.

Amanda carried Genevieve upstairs to her crib, pulled the curtains, and took the baby monitor back down. Her thoughts hummed like a speedboat. She hadn't seen Sam look like that in ages—maybe not since the car accident they'd been in together nearly two years ago. She focused on her breathing so as not to start shaking. She had to stay calm.

Sam sat at the kitchen table with a stack of papers in front of him and his head bowed. He looked defeated. Amanda sat beside him, and Sam slid the stack over to her so she could read it. Her heart dropped into her stomach.

They were closing the Sunrise Cove Inn. Effective immediately.

"They can't do this, can they?" Sam demanded. "Tell me they can't do this."

"Let me read," Amanda said, trying to keep her voice normal. "Why don't you make yourself a cup of tea? Relax a little?"

Sam was on his feet. He cut across the kitchen and retrieved a beer from the fridge. After he popped the tab, he drained half of it, his Adam's apple bouncing. Amanda tried to focus on the words in front of her to make sense of the legal terminology that had come second nature before she'd begun to doubt herself. She knew Sam wanted her to find a reason this wasn't legal so he could throw it back in the State of Massachusetts's face.

But Amanda was struck with how airtight the paperwork was. Due to the potential weight of history in the basement, they wanted to preserve the Sunrise Cove Inn as best as they could. They didn't want to put it at the mercy of any guests eager to pry or destroy it, either on accident or on purpose.

"I don't like the look on your face," Sam said from the fridge.

Amanda raised her eyes. She didn't smile. "I don't think you can fight this. Not yet anyway."

Sam's hand clenched in a fist. He staggered to the counter and stared at his shoes for a long time. The beer hung sadly in his other hand.

Amanda had a strange thought. All this had happened so quickly. It was just one day after they'd learned of the potential of that downstairs room. It twisted her up inside. Was it possible that the Arnouts had had a hand in this, too? That they'd decided to go after her husband's career rather than just her own? They had ties with the governor that surely allowed them wonderful relations with the Historical Society of Massachusetts. All the governor had to do was make a call.

If the Arnouts were really behind this, they were craftier than she'd thought. There was an entire legal arena that involved protecting historical sites. They were using everything they could.

Amanda had poked the bear. And now he was hungry for blood.

Amanda shook her head of her suspicions. Regardless of whether this was the fault of the Arnouts or not, she had to help Sam.

"We need to get everyone out of the Sunrise Cove immediately," Amanda said firmly. "If we don't, they could fine us thousands of dollars."

They couldn't afford that. Not after the desolate winter they'd had. Not if tourist season wasn't a given. Amanda shivered at the implications of this closure.

Sam tugged his hair. "I don't know what to do. Where can we put them?"

Amanda's head thudded. "How many guests do you have right now?"

"We're more than half full," Sam said. "Six rooms. One of them is a family, so they'll need two beds and a cot." He groaned. "I could call around the island. See if anyone has rooms. But we can't afford to put everyone up for the remainder of their vacations."

Amanda shot toward her cell and grabbed it without telling Sam what was on her mind. The phone rang out across the island before the answer.

"Amanda! This is a surprise."

"Hi, Aunt Kelli," Amanda said with a smile. Kelli wasn't officially her "aunt," but she grouped all the Montgomery siblings as second-tier aunts and uncles rather than second cousins. "How are you?"

"I'm doing well. I just spoke to my mom on the phone about all that madness at the Sunrise Cove. She's beside herself. She wants to get in the basement."

Amanda shivered with fake laughter. Sam watched her from the kitchen and nodded along. He'd caught on.

"That's sort of why I'm calling," Amanda said. "The State of Massachusetts is shutting us down for the time being. It's so sudden, and we don't know what to do with our guests."

Kelli balked. "They are not! I can't believe this. That soon?"

"I'm afraid so."

Kelli sputtered. "Let me talk to Piper." Piper was the manager of the Aquinnah Cliffside Overlook Hotel, whom Kelli had put mostly in charge after she'd worked herself to the bone last summer. Kelli now enjoyed the fruits of owning a gorgeous hotel without the stress of managing the details.

Amanda and Sam waited in stunned silence. Three minutes went by before Kelli returned.

"Piper says we have five rooms available here at the hotel," Kelli said.

Amanda breathed a sigh of relief. "Five rooms? That's incredible."

"They're available for the next five days," Kelli said. "Lucky for you, it's not quite tourist season yet."

"I can't thank you enough, Kelli," Amanda said. "I'll call you when we're on our way."

Sam and Amanda were blurry with confusion and gratefulness. Amanda hurried upstairs to put Genevieve in the baby carrier and grab her supplies before meeting

Sam in the car and speeding back to the Sunrise Cove. They found Grandpa Wes at the front desk. He was gray and nervous, answering the guests' questions as best he could. He looked on the brink of tears.

He'd never had to close the Sunrise Cove Inn. He hadn't even closed it when Anna Sheridan died.

Amanda hugged her grandfather and reminded him that this was only temporary. "As soon as they get organized at the Historical Society, I'm sure they'll let us re-open. I'll badger them about it this week."

"That's my lawyer," Grandpa Wes said. "You're a fighter, Amanda. I'm so glad you're on our side."

Amanda's chest heaved with the truth. She wasn't necessarily a lawyer right now. Everything felt volatile and out of her control.

It was five thirty, which meant many guests were returning from exploring the island to get ready for dinner. Sam stood in the foyer to greet guests coming back and explain the situation. Amanda didn't wait around to hear them groan and ask questions. She darted down the hall to the bistro to find Zach and Christine in the kitchen. Christine pulled out a tray of cookies as she entered, blasting her with a scrumptious, chocolatey smell.

"Amanda! So glad you're here. You have to taste my cookies," Christine said.

Amanda would have done anything to sit down, gossip with her aunt Christine, and eat a load of cookies. But she was blurry and on the move.

She explained everything as quickly as she could. They had to close down the Sunrise Cove and the bistro. They couldn't serve food here at all. Nobody could be on the premises save for the historians and their appointed crew.

Christine's jaw dropped. "You've got to be kidding me."

Zach looked especially panicked. "Do they know how slim our profit margins are? Do they know that all restaurants are always on the brink of collapse?" He hit the counter with a spatula. "Haven't they even seen The Bear?"

Christine touched Zach's shoulder and whispered, "Let's get everything out of the fridge and freeze what we can. Maybe we can take some stuff to the food kitchen."

Christine flinched as Amanda prepared to leave. "What time do you need us out?"

"By tonight," Amanda said before she disappeared through the swiveling kitchen door.

Amanda found Sam in a heated discussion with three couples in the foyer. Two of them she recognized as bird-watchers she'd seen on the shoreline near the harbor.

"Trust me," Sam said, "you'll love the Aquinnah Cliff-side Overlook. It's a truly remarkable hotel. Far more expensive than this one. And incredibly historical!" He tried to laugh, then bit his lip. His charm was fading with all this panic.

"If it's historical, why wasn't it closed down, too?" one of the guests asked.

"There's a lot I don't understand about this either," Sam said. "I'm flying by the seat of my pants. But I hope you'll bear with me as we get through this. You can stay at the Aquinnah free of charge for the remainder of your vacation. And I hope you'll contact me personally if you need anything in particular."

The couples exchanged glances and shrugged.

"When do you need us out?" a man asked.

"As soon as possible," Sam said. "If you could be out of your rooms and headed to the Aquinnah Cliffside in the next two hours, that would be fantastic. If you stay beyond tonight, there's a high probability that we'll face a fine."

"It doesn't seem legal," one of the women said.

Sam's face was flushed. Amanda looked down at the baby sleeping in her carrier near the greeting counter. She looked so blissful, so immune to the chaos around her.

With the three couples up in their rooms to pack, Amanda and Sam had to hunt down the others. Because the Aquinnah couldn't accommodate the family of four, Sam and Amanda had agreed to offer up their private home while they stayed at the Sheridan House with Audrey, Noah, and Max. Audrey was over the moon despite the circumstances. She saw it as a sleepover with her best friend.

Before the family of four arrived, Amanda hurried home to clean up and change all the sheets in the house. She considered it insanity that her baby was fifteen days old and required to sleep elsewhere. Everyone knew that these were precious days; everything came down to your comfort and your baby's comfort. But these were difficult and very strange times. Maybe she and Sam would look back on them fondly one day. "Remember when we almost lost the Sunrise Cove?" They would get through by the skin of their teeth.

The couple and their three children arrived around seven thirty. Amanda was there to greet them and show them to their rooms: the married couple in Amanda and Sam's bed; two of the children in the guest bedroom;

another on the pull-out couch. The family was from Ohio and very far from home.

"We would have just gone home if it was closer," the wife said apologetically.

Amanda got the sense that they'd scrimped and saved for this vacation, so going home early would have broken their hearts. She was grateful to be able to open her home to these people. But before she left them behind, she made sure to put all the valuables in a safe and twist it locked.

These days, she couldn't trust anyone except her family.

Chapter Fifteen

The move from the Sunrise Cove Inn to the Aquinnah Cliffside Overlook was as fluid as it could be, given the circumstances. All five of the rooms were occupied with Sunrise Cove guests by eight thirty that night, and by nine, they'd gathered in the ornate ballroom for drinks to discuss the "craziness" of the day. Amanda sat a few tables away from them and thought, *You don't even know the half of it.*

Genevieve was fast asleep in Kelli's office down the hall. Amanda had set up a baby monitor and was prepared to flee the table at the first sign she was needed. But right now, she sat with Aunt Kelli, her mother, and Audrey, drinking rosé and discussing the chaos of the day. Grandpa Wes and Sam were back at the Sunrise Cove, ensuring all loose ends were tied up. Amanda was glad they were together. The world felt off-kilter and prepared for collapse.

"And there's really no way out of this? No loophole?" Aunt Kelli asked softly.

Amanda shook her head. "I've gone over the paperwork ten times. I even pulled out one of my old law text-books to read up on state law regarding historical sites. They're completely within their right to do this."

Susan groaned and met Amanda's gaze. "You really think it's the Arnouts?"

Amanda had mentioned her theory that the Arnout family might be involved in the sudden closure of the Sunrise Cove Inn.

"I probably sound paranoid," Amanda said.

"You don't," Susan said.

Audrey's eyebrows rose. "The Arnouts? You mean that Nantucket family?"

Amanda's heart stopped beating for a second. Was she ready to confess her dark secret—that she'd lost her license to practice law? Was she ready to admit she'd lost her identity?

Amanda raised her left shoulder. "They're stirring up trouble for me right now. We don't know for sure if they're behind it, but it seems likely." She took a long, boorish drink of wine. "I made Mr. Arnout very angry recently. I sent him an email I shouldn't have. And I have a hunch that he saw the Sunrise Cove's historical site broadcasted on the news and decided to make my life even more miserable."

Audrey's eyes stirred with questions. As a journalist, she was accustomed to putting puzzle pieces together.

"It's because of them that my license to practice law was suspended," Amanda added with a sigh.

Audrey and Aunt Kelli gasped.

"They can't just take it away like that!" Audrey cried. "After all you've done? All that hard work?"

"They can, and they did," Amanda said firmly.

"But we're going to get it back." Susan clenched her fists over the table.

"And this is all because they don't think their son did anything wrong?" Audrey asked.

"They think I mishandled the case, yes," Amanda said.

Audrey's mouth hung open. "Why didn't they just represent him themselves, then? Or make a call in the first place that would make his legal troubles disappear?"

Susan made a sound in her throat and took a long drink of wine.

"What?" Audrey asked.

Aunt Kelli sniffed. "They had him on CCTV, didn't they? The entire world knows he did what he did." She turned to look Amanda in the eye. "Let me get this straight. The parents are angry with you for not getting their kid a not-guilty verdict? When it was literally an impossible task?"

Amanda winced. "When I first took on the case, Mom and I talked about expectations with the Arnouts," she remembered. "We reminded them that our job was to whittle the sentence down from five to eight years to one or two."

"Mr. Arnout looked like he blew a fuse," Susan remembered.

"Which isn't uncommon in situations like that," Amanda said. "People don't like to hear that prison is a given. But I figured they'd come around to it, especially after the trial. They spent hours listening to the prosecution's witnesses, hearing about their evidence, and watching the CCTV footage. And they still came away with the ever-loving belief that their son is an angel."

"They should be studied by psychologists," Audrey

scoffed. A split second later, her face melted, and she added, "Although it would be horrible to learn that Max had done something so heinous. I can't pretend to know what my brain would do in that case. Maybe I wouldn't be able to accept it either."

"But you wouldn't use your time, connections, and resources to ruin the lawyer's life," Susan pointed out.

"No. I would hide myself in a cave and never come out," Audrey said.

* * *

Amanda could recite Hilton Arnout's case verbatim. Probably she always could, now that it was the case that had rocked her life like a tsunami to a fishing boat.

A rich playboy with too much time on his hands, Hilton had spent his years after graduating from Harvard traveling all over the world. He'd spent months in Thailand, Japan, and Bali. He'd sunk a yacht—on accident or on purpose, it wasn't clear—outside Istanbul. He'd gotten married once to an Indian princess in Mumbai and then left her two weeks after the grand affair with a French model who looked vaguely like Brigitte Bardot. It was said he was so hated in India that her father would immediately have him killed if he ever returned. This seemed to only add fuel to the fire that was Hilton Arnout.

It wasn't clear exactly why Hilton returned to Harvard for graduate school. Amanda guessed his father had pitched it to him as a good idea. Maybe he wanted him to have the credentials to take over the Arnout money and businesses one day. Perhaps he just wanted Hilton to calm down a little bit.

At twenty-four, Hilton returned to Harvard as a graduate student in International Relations. He lived in a gorgeous three-story Victorian near campus that was soon widely known as the party spot. Only the most beautiful undergraduate girls and the most promising graduate men could attend—plus Hilton's wide array of friends who came from other cities and countries to have the "college party experience." It was presumed that Hilton met Caitlin Carson at one of these parties. She was twenty years old, blond, with very long legs and very bright teeth, and always in attendance. She sort of looked like Brigitte Bardot, too. Hilton clearly had a type.

Hilton limped his way through his first semesters of graduate school. According to the Harvard professors Amanda had interviewed as she'd prepared for the case, Hilton hardly did anything toward his graduate degree. The dean put pressure on the professors to ensure that Hilton passed. "Everyone knew who he was and what his connections were," a female professor explained to Amanda. "Tenured professors were too frightened to get on the dean's bad side, and non-tenured professors didn't have a choice at all. We had to smile and joke with Hilton. We were all in it."

But everything changed at the end of the second semester. Caitlin Carson's grades suffered (presumably because of those wild parties), and the dean threatened to kick her out of school. He did not know that Caitlin and Hilton were in love, nor that Hilton's brand of love bordered on obsession. He was always "all in, or all out."

"When Caitlin came to him crying one afternoon, I knew something was up," a male ex-friend of Hilton's explained to Amanda via email. "He had this fire in his eyes I'll never forget. I suggested he just call the dean to, you know, explain that Caitlin was his girlfriend. I figured that would calm everything down. The dean would retract his threat, you know? But instead, Hilton got it in his head that he wanted to punish the dean. I think he'd seen too many films. Maybe he wanted to prove himself to Caitlin. He was feeling old and stupid. He knew he was only getting through grad school because everyone feared his father and the dean."

On the night of May 21, 2023, Hilton Arnout and Caitlin Carson broke into the dean's house at 11:32 p.m. The date and time were known because of CCTV footage; it would always be drilled into Amanda's brain.

It wasn't clear exactly why Hilton wanted Caitlin to come with him. Amanda's theory was that he needed someone to see just how wild he was about to get. He needed a witness. And what better witness than his girlfriend?

It was also known that Hilton and Caitlin were very drunk and high on drugs at the time of the break-in. Witnesses had seen them doing Molly and coke before ducking out into the night.

Hilton didn't wait long before breaking something. He smashed three multi-thousand-dollar vases in the foyer and used the dust to write terrible words across the floor. Caitlin laughed and goaded him on. After that, they went to the dining room, the living room, and the bedroom to destroy more property, pour water on technological equipment, and throw things out the window. More than one million dollars in damages was recorded— an impressive feat for one guy walking through a house with his girlfriend.

But when they reached the dean's "game room," the story shifted. The dean was a collector of ancient weapons, including Grecian javelins, old stone tips, a basilisk cannon, and many samurai swords. Hilton had handled samurai swords in Japan and was a collector of sorts. He brandished one of them excitedly—out of his mind with drugs—and swooshed it around. Caitlin wasn't prepared and didn't jump out of the way in time. And suddenly, blood was everywhere. He'd gotten her on the upper arm and the lower stomach. All of the neighbors reported hearing her screams at 1:10 a.m. It was incredible that they'd already been in the house for nearly two hours by that point. Two hours of destruction.

The cops and ambulance arrived a few minutes later. They bolted through the chaos of the dean's house to find Caitlin passed out in Hilton's arms and blood everywhere. They immediately arrested Hilton and took Caitlin to the hospital. The dean was called. He was vacationing on Nantucket—with Hilton's parents, ironically enough. He was back by morning.

Caitlin did not die, thank goodness. She didn't even lose her arm. She spent several weeks in the hospital, where her parents refused to let her see Hilton Arnout. By then, Hilton's father had bailed him out and contacted the "top defense attorney" on the East Coast, Susan Sheridan. Overloaded with casework, Susan roped in her daughter, Amanda, calling her "the best of the best."

"You have to understand," Mr. Arnout had told Amanda over the phone. "Our son is a victim of a horrible witch hunt."

Amanda was accustomed to people's delusions when it came to cases and their or their loved one's criminality. But the Arnouts had surprised her with their certainty. It was as though they lived on another planet. For them, Hilton was not guilty, not in the least. The CCTV was doctored. Everyone was after their wealth and power. Period.

However, the Arnouts didn't account for the power of Caitlin's family. Caitlin Carson was a Harvard undergrad for reasons similar to Hilton's. Her father knew people who knew people. And the prosecution attacked Hilton from all angles—regarding his dramatic history, his lack of respect for others' property, and his attempt at the manslaughter of Caitlin Carson. The fact that he was a great deal older than Caitlin was—in a position of power when compared to her—did nothing to help their case.

It was actually incredible that Amanda had been able to knock the sentence down to a year.

A part of her felt guilty for that. Hilton was the sort of man who belonged behind bars for a lot longer. He was a menace to himself and others. And it seemed clear that the minute he left prison, he would be back to his old tricks again. Caitlin wouldn't be his only victim. But that was the nature of the criminal justice system. Very rich people could get away with a whole lot, while very poor people could hardly pickpocket a wallet without doing time.

The kitchen light glowed through the darkness, and Sam's car was in the driveway. Amanda braced herself. There was no telling what kind of mood he'd be in. She wanted to be supportive no matter what.

Susan squeezed Amanda's wrist. "We have to stay strong."

"We always do." But Amanda's voice wavered. Everything was off.

Amanda carried Genevieve inside quietly. Susan helped her with the diaper bag and the carrier, which she set down in the foyer before hugging her and backing out into the night. Amanda watched her mother's car lights purr down the dark road and disappear around the bend, thinking about how she'd listened to her mother's footfalls disappear up the hallway after she'd said good night so many years ago. A youthful part of her ached to have those years back.

"Hello?" Sam's voice was weak.

Amanda left Genevieve asleep in her carrier in the foyer and tiptoed to the kitchen. Sam hunkered over the table with a glass of whiskey and a bag of chips. He looked up at her, his eyes bloodshot. Amanda poured him a glass of water and rubbed his back. His sigh was that of a very old man.

"It's going to be okay," Amanda said. "We got everyone out of the Sunrise Cove in time. That was step one. We'll just take it one day at a time."

Sam rubbed his temples. "I've spent all night running the numbers. It doesn't look good."

Amanda's heartbeat felt syncopated.

"It was a dismal winter," Sam said. "We just didn't bring in the revenue we needed to. We have quite a few reservations over the next few weeks, but we'll probably have to refund all that money. And we'll have to do it sooner rather than later so that people can make other plans. But we just don't have the money to refund everyone. Not right now. I've already paid the construction company for their work on the basement—work that they can't complete. And if we aren't open for tourist season..." He sighed. "We're doomed, Amanda."

Amanda collapsed in the chair beside him. She was too exhausted to speak.

"Your family entrusted this inn to me," Sam said. "I would hate myself forever if I let it die."

"It's not your fault," Amanda breathed. In her mind's eye, she imagined a faceless corporation bulldozing the Sunrise Cove Inn and building a high-rise luxury apartment complex for rich tourists who planned to swarm the beaches. She shuddered.

Sam wouldn't accept the fact that this wasn't his fault. To him, he hadn't paid close enough attention to the cash flow throughout the autumn and winter. He hadn't brought in enough tourism during Christmas. He hadn't laid down his life enough for the inn. The devastation etched on his face broke Amanda's heart in two.

Her thoughts raced, searching tirelessly for an answer. It felt like her brain was eating itself.

"We're going to get through this," Amanda assured him, a platitude so empty that it echoed.

Sam blinked at her and opened his palms to the sky. "How?" he asked.

"Just give me some time to think," she said.

But Amanda had no idea where to turn. Perhaps he was right. Maybe it was too late.

Chapter Sixteen

W es returned home at ten o'clock that evening to find Tommy Gasbarro at the kitchen table with a bottle of beer. Tommy's lips were in a thin line. Wes wavered in the doorway and blinked at him, unable to fully admit that he hadn't recognized Tommy when he'd first walked in. He'd thought there was an intruder casually drinking beer at the kitchen table. He reminded himself to smile.

"Hey, Tommy. This is a surprise."

Tommy was Beatrice's only real family on the island. Tommy was married to Lola. He was also related to Stan Ellis—a fact that Wes tried to blot out of his mind. Why could he forget everything else but this?

Tommy sipped his beer. "Beatrice is asleep."

Wes nodded and sat at the table. He avoided drinking like the plague, as it made his already foggy mind even grayer, but right now, Tommy's beer looked perfect: golden and crisp and so calming. It had been one heck of a day.

"Did you get any of Beatrice's phone calls?" Tommy asked.

Wes was stricken. He touched the pocket where he normally kept his phone but found only his keys. Perhaps he'd left his phone at the Sunrise Cove in all the chaos.

"I guess I didn't," Wes said, knocking his forehead with his knuckles. "Did she need something?"

"She had a doctor's appointment at four thirty," Tommy said. "She mentioned reminding you about it this morning. You were supposed to take her."

Wes felt the words like a javelin through his chest. He coughed and removed his ledger from his bag. On today's date, he'd written: "BEATRICE DOCTOR @ 4:30!" It had gone out of his head like clouds buzzing across the sky and out of sight.

Wes rubbed his temples so hard that he saw spots. "I should have been here." He couldn't even remember what kind of doctor it was. Gynecologist? Heart? Although Wes's health was worse by a thousand degrees, Beatrice had her own situations to deal with. She'd stuck by Wes tirelessly, helping him arrange his life so that his dementia didn't unravel it too quickly. She'd even chased him while he'd sleepwalked and ensured he didn't leap in the sound.

What kind of partner was he?

Tommy cleared his throat. "I know today was chaotic up at the Cove," he said. "Lola just called and explained everything."

"It's no excuse for missing this," Wes said.

Tommy palmed the back of his neck and gave Wes a look that made Wes feel one hundred years older than he was. The look seemed to ask: *are you sure you're up to the task of marrying her? Are you sure you can be trusted?*

Wes could have died of embarrassment and sorrow on the spot. He wanted to tell Tommy that *nobody told you what it's really like to get old. How debilitating it is. How embarrassing it is to forget.* But he knew there was no reaching through the years that separated them to explain himself. Tommy would always see Wes as a very old and sick man until he, too, was a very old and sick man. By then, Wes would be gone.

Tommy drained his beer and rinsed it in the sink. "She has new medication on the counter. Make sure she takes it in the morning, please."

Wes wrote in his ledger: "Beatrice - new medication - take it!" He clicked the end of his pen nervously. He wanted Tommy to leave.

Tommy paused at the counter. "They closed up the Cove, then?"

"For now," Wes said. It felt like there was a brick on his chest. "But Susan and Amanda are on the case. I can't imagine we'll be closed down for long."

Tommy sucked in his cheeks. "I thought that secret room was a blessing. It feels more like a curse, doesn't it?"

Wes didn't know what to say. Tommy approached from the side and tapped his shoulder before passing through the foyer and saying, "Good night." From the kitchen table, Wes could hear the screech of Tommy's tires. He couldn't remember having seen his truck when he'd gotten home. Maybe he'd parked around the side.

Wes padded gently down the hallway and peered through the shadows at Beatrice's sleeping form. She looked so gentle and beautiful with her white hair spilled across the pillow. Wes wanted to burrow against her and cry into her shoulder. He wanted to pray to God to make them both young and healthy. He imagined what kind of child they might have had. Maybe a boy—someone similar to Sam. A family man who would have held the weight of the Sunrise Cove with tenderness and love.

Wes hardly slept that night. He stared through the darkness, listening to Beatrice breathing and imagining a world in which the Sunrise Cove Inn didn't exist. He'd sensed this possibility in the heaviness of Sam's language. "I just don't know what we're going to do," he'd muttered.

The Sunrise Cove had been Wes's life, which meant he was one of the only people in the world who understood how essential the first few weeks of spring and summer were to the yearly revenue. Anna had said those weeks were like "free falling." She'd sang the Tom Petty song continually, her eyes manic. "We made it," she'd always said when the revenue had balanced out again. "We live to open the Sunrise Cove doors another day."

Wes got up early to make Beatrice an enormous breakfast. He cracked eggs, stirred pancakes, set out fresh fruit, and made heart-healthy sausages in the skillet. He brewed coffee and turned on the radio, where a weatherman said today would be in the high sixties. "Another gorgeous day in the East." The radio DJ played all the hits from the sixties, seventies, and eighties. Wes bounced around, energized, and reminded himself, over and over again, that Dr. Hamilton would soon allow him to start on the brand-new dementia medication. Maybe soon, he would be free.

"What's all this?" Beatrice smiled sweetly and walked over to wrap her arms around him.

Wes's heart banged. "I wanted to treat you," he said, hugging her. "I'm just so sorry I missed your appointment yesterday."

Beatrice's smile didn't fade. She swatted her hand

around and poured herself a cup of coffee. "Don't think about it for a second. I know all about the Sunrise Cove. You must be heartbroken."

Wes flinched. "Don't let me off the hook. I should have been here."

Beatrice went onto her tiptoes to kiss him on the cheek and lips. "I hope Tommy didn't give you a hard time. You know how he can be."

"He's right."

Beatrice rolled her eyes.

"You need to take your new medication!" Wes cried a little too loudly. He reached for the package and passed it to her.

Beatrice took the package. She probably hadn't forgotten but just hadn't gotten to it yet. "Thank you for remembering. That's very sweet."

Wes smiled and filled her plate with eggs, pancakes, and sausage, then ordered her to sit down. He'd read the package and knew she needed to take the medicine with food.

He wanted to be a good husband to her. He wanted to be there for the good days, the bad days, and the boring days. He wanted to remember every detail for as long as he could.

And a part of that, for now, was faking how well he was doing. "Fake it till you make it" had become his internal mantra. Their wedding day was fast approaching. He planned to enjoy—and remember—every second.

Chapter Seventeen

The first several days after the Sunrise Cove shuttered its doors were monstrous. Genevieve refused to sleep for longer than two hours at a time, which meant that Amanda was up and down and up and down, never reaching REM sleep and hardly taking time to wash her hair or cook herself a healthy meal. She felt frayed at the edges. Sam was around to help when he could, but he spent most of his days dealing with Sunrise Cove logistics and talking to the historians about what they knew thus far and when they thought he could re-open. It was like watching a caged animal try to flee. It was impossible.

Audrey and Max came over to distract Amanda often. Amanda adored them to bits, but Max's toddler mania had reached a peak, and his screams often rattled through her and left her ears ringing. Audrey cooked for her and helped her clean up around the house, which made Amanda joke, "Look at us! The tables have turned." But Audrey's cleanliness wasn't even close to Amanda's, which meant she always had to re-do it after Audrey left.

This made her feel ungrateful and also high maintenance. Would anything feel normal again?

Five days after the Sunrise Cove closed, Amanda received a call from her mother. Amanda could see Susan at the law office, her posture statuesque as she said, "I'm thinking of sending a cease and desist. Bruce thinks it's a good idea."

Bruce Holland was another criminal justice lawyer at their law office.

Amanda groaned. "I don't think anything will work against these people. It feels like the Arnouts are above the law."

"Hilton is in prison," Susan reminded her. "We just have to get creative about how we protect ourselves from the other Arnouts."

Amanda was stretched across the sofa, flicking through television stations and streaming sites and killing time until Genevieve woke up again. She sensed it coming like a storm.

It wasn't like Amanda to laze around like this in front of the television. She remembered telling Audrey that TV "rotted people's minds." Why didn't Audrey smack her? Past Amanda was so annoying! She had no idea how difficult it was to raise a baby!

"Are you holding up okay?" Susan's voice switched from lawyer tone to mother tone in a second flat.

"Yeah. I'm fine." Amanda's voice wavered.

"You don't sound fine. Can I bring you anything? You want a burrito for dinner? I can stop by your favorite place."

When had Amanda become the sort of woman to yearn for a burrito as though it was the secret to happiness? She closed her eyes and groaned.

"How is Sam?"

"He's bad," Amanda answered honestly. "He's working so hard to get the inn back up and running."

"You told him about the Arnouts?"

"Not really. I don't think telling him there's no use in trying would help anything," Amanda said. "I don't want him to feel hopeless."

"Does that mean you feel hopeless?"

Amanda rolled her tongue across the back of her teeth and wondered when she'd last flossed. "I don't know."

Susan gave her a brief pep talk about the benefits of eating, showering, and getting outside "where the sun was shining" to ensure better mental health, then had to get off the phone to tend to a client. "I'm coming over later," she announced. "Whether you let me in or not."

This was the kind of tough love Susan Sheridan offered others in spades. Amanda half remembered it from more than three years ago— after Chris had left her at the altar and she'd spent a period of time moaning in bed. Where was Chris now? Amanda gave in to her reckless tendencies to stalk Chris on Instagram and see that, apparently, he'd bought a house in Greece and had a very beautiful blond girlfriend and a shaggy dog. They beamed from tiny squares on her phone, seeming to say, "We have no problems!"

Amanda threw her phone to the far edge of the couch and continued to flick through the stations. She wound up on The HISTORY Channel, her father's favorite. An older man walked through what had once been the battleground of Gettysburg with his fingers laced together and spoke about the "bloody battle" and its ramifications during the Civil War.

Suddenly a gong went through Amanda's head. She bolted to her feet and stared at the man on-screen.

Off the top of her head, she could name twelve people borderline-obsessed with the Civil War in her life. Her father. Her grandfather. Uncle Steve. Uncle Trevor. Others she'd met in law school. Others she'd gone to undergrad with. The Civil War was the storied horror that had once cratered through this great nation and kept them apart.

If Sam's hunch was correct, the secret room beneath the Sunrise Cove was a part of that history. People needed to see it. They needed to learn about the dramatic history of the Underground Railroad on Martha's Vineyard. And maybe Amanda could be the one to bring it to them.

Amanda fled the living room to find her laptop beneath a stack of old books and unused diapers. It was remarkable how unused the laptop was now that she had no reason to work her brain. She immediately googled Cynthia Brighton, then tapped her leg with one hand as she scouted through Cynthia's LinkedIn page and her new law office in Los Angeles for contact details. Cynthia was an entertainment lawyer who'd handled numerous documentaries for HBO, The HISTORY Channel, and Hulu. Did she know the right people to get this going?

Amanda and Cynthia went way back. They'd originally met in undergrad at a pep rally they hadn't wanted to be at. Amanda was there with Chris; Cynthia was there with a jock she was dating at the time. They'd spent an hour screaming at each other over the sound of the pep rally about why they loved law so much. Their friendship was solidified. But Amanda hadn't understood why Cynthia had wanted to go into entertainment law of all things. To her, it was the crassest of law arenas. Why didn't she want to help people and deal with real-life cases?

The answer was money, of course. It always came down to that. And right now, Amanda needed money more than anything to keep the Sunrise Cove alive.

Amanda wrote a polite and professional-sounding email. She didn't want to seem too cozy with Cynthia, as they hadn't kept up with each other after Amanda had moved to Martha's Vineyard full-time and taken law classes online. She'd sort of abandoned her friends and replaced them with her Sheridan family. She didn't regret it, but it came with professional consequences.

In the email, Amanda suggested that one of Cynthia's clients might want to document the "exciting new historical site on Martha's Vineyard and analyze the dramatic history of the Underground Railroad on the island itself." It was amazing bait. People across the United States loved the idea of Martha's Vineyard; loved the long stretches of white beaches, the lighthouses, the fishing boats, and the wealth of the celebrity tourists. The fact that its history went so far back was illuminating. It activated the imagination.

Amanda was so excited about her idea. She felt restored. She vacuumed the living room, scrubbed the kitchen counters, then prepared a feast of salmon, greens, and sweet potato fries for dinner. She even popped a bottle of wine that she'd been saving for Thanksgiving or Christmas. When Sam stumbled into the house, world-weary and gaunt, his eyes stirred with confusion.

"What's all this about?"

Amanda threw her arms around Sam and said, "I don't know if it will work. But hear me out."

Over dinner, Amanda explained everything. Sam listened intently, ate his salmon, and nodded; his eyebrows furrowed. When Amanda said she'd already reached out to Cynthia, he raised his lips into a near-smile. It was the first Amanda had seen in days. It felt like the sun.

"It seems like it really was used for the Underground Railroad," Sam admitted, wiping his mouth with a napkin. "The guys downstairs finally showed me some photos when they finished up today."

Sam had taken photographs of their photographs. They showed the dark room with its two beds, bunk bed, cabinets, the baby crib, and trunk from numerous angles, plus personal items: a very old comb, a home-made teddy bear, and a few other items that, apparently, were used as "baby supplies." Amanda didn't recognize them as anything used today.

"It seems likely that Wes's great-great-grandfather was instrumental in setting up this safe room for the Railroad," Sam explained, parroting what he'd learned.

"My great-great-great-great-grandfather, you mean," Amanda said with a smile.

"Exactly." Sam swiped through his photos to show an old black-and-white family portrait of a man, a woman, and four children. The man had a thick black beard and kind eyes, and the children looked to be between the ages of one and seven. The wife was stern and sad-looking. Amanda could only imagine why. One baby was no picnic, so four, far before the era of microwaves and baby monitors, must have killed her.

Amanda was living in the easiest era it had ever been to be a woman, and she still struggled to survive.

"This is him," Sam explained. "Matthew Sheridan,

his wife Wendy, and their children, Randolph, Anna, Henry, and Nadia. It seems like he bought a camera around 1862 or 1863 and really enjoyed taking portraits. Many of the ex-slaves stayed with him, which was really risky if you think about it. He was literally recording his crime."

Sam brought up several more photographs. They were all of the Black people who'd fled the South and sought freedom in the North. The Black women and men looked far skinnier and gaunter than the Sheridan family. Their eyes were sorrowful, and their clothing was often torn and ratty.

One thought rang through Amanda. In taking their photograph, Matthew Sheridan had given them a place in history. He'd made it known that they mattered to him as people.

In all, thirty individual photographs were discovered in the trunk downstairs. Mr. Sheridan had apparently hidden them.

"But something else was in the trunk," Sam declared. "A diary."

Amanda's eyes widened.

"Unfortunately, it's way too delicate to handle on-site," Sam said. "One of the historians is taking it to a lab to read over it and record everything he finds. It'll open the window to that time period and into Matthew Sheridan's life. It's astonishing."

It truly was. Amanda collapsed back in the chair beside Sam, reeling. The past felt like a tremendously heavy thing. Her plight as a "new mom" seemed so laughable now.

More than that, thinking of a young mother—or multiple young mothers—in the basement floored her.

"None of the photos had babies, did they?"

"None that they showed me," Sam said.

Amanda chewed her lip. "I'm sure Cynthia will want to know all about this. I'll email her right away."

But when Amanda pulled up her email, Cynthia had already written back. She'd already heard about the discoveries beneath the Sunrise Cove and had been thinking of reaching out to Wes Sheridan. "Are you related to him?"

Amanda wrote back immediately to say that she and her husband were now more or less in charge of the inn. She didn't want to burden her grandfather with the horror of their current expenses. She wanted to sweep this stress under the rug and plunge into HISTORY Channel wealth.

"Let's set up a call," Cynthia said in her email. "I hope we get to work together again!"

Upstairs, Genevieve woke up again and rattled with cries. Amanda bolted to tend to her, feeling stronger and more awake than she had all week. When Genevieve saw her, Amanda half imagined that she smiled at her—a real smile that was definitely not possible this early in Genevieve's life. But real smiles were coming. Amanda couldn't wait.

Chapter Eighteen

From the Diary of Martha Smith
April 1, 1864

Mrs. Sheridan just shared a wonderful truth with me. The island—this island—has a name. And that name is my name. It's *Martha. Martha's Vineyard.* Truly, this made me laugh for so long and so hard that I thought the slave owners in the South would hear me and send their dogs after me. But when I calmed down, it was just me, Mrs. Sheridan, and baby Mary in the basement. It was just us, same as it usually is, on this island that has borne my name for longer than I've been alive. A lot longer.

It's hard to believe so much time has gone by. I can smell the difference; I can practically hear the trees and flowers and grass growing outside, stretching up to what must be the bluest of blue skies. Mrs. Sheridan keeps saying we need to find a way to get me and the baby out there; that it's not good for a baby to be cooped up inside *her whole life. But we both know it's too risky. In fact, in order to protect me, Mr. and Mrs. Sheridan stopped accepting new escapers. They don't put the lantern out anymore. I feel complicated about this. But we have to keep the baby safe.*

April 3, 1864

I had another dream about Virgil and Jane. They were safe in Canada, and they knew they needed to reach out to me. But when Jane sat down to write a letter, she remembered she didn't know how to write. There was no way to contact me. She wept.

I woke up in the basement in a cold sweat. The baby was crying, and I did my best to calm her even as I cried, too. I try to remember what it's like to feel the sun on your cheeks and the grass between your toes. I try to remember what it's like to have Virgil's strong arms around me. But all of that is fading.

May 2, 1864

It was the most beautiful night of my life.

After darkness blanketed the island, Mrs. Sheridan came downstairs, opened the trapdoor, and said, "Martha, won't you please join us for dinner?" I thought maybe it was a trap. I was terrified. But Mrs. Sheridan's face was as warm and inviting as ever. And I thought at that moment that if I spend another second in this basement, I'll die. So I followed her.

To my surprise, all the Sheridan children were seated at the table: Randolph and Henry and Anna and Nadia. They peered at me curiously—the way white children do to colored people—but they weren't unkind. There was a plate already made up for me at the table. They asked me to sit.

The dinner was the best of my life. I tried to hold myself back from eating it all at once. There were carrots and mushrooms; there was fish with mustard sauce; there were mashed potatoes. When I scraped my plate clean, Mrs. Sheridan put more food on it. I couldn't believe it. Tears spilled from my eyes.

Mr. Sheridan told his children about the "tremendous hardship" I'd been through, and that I was safe with them. He explained how important it was never to tell anyone about me. I flinched with fear. How could you trust children with such an enormous secret? But they took it to heart and nodded along and crossed their hearts. They spoke of God as though they could feel him in the room with us. For the first time in a while, I felt him, too.

May 11, 1864

Tonight was the first time I was allowed outside. I put Mary on a blanket beneath the sprawling starry sky and listened to the wind rush through the trees and the waves crash on the shore. I was quiet for nearly an hour before Mrs. Sheridan interrupted my thoughts. She asked me if I thought often of my sister and husband. I said yes, every day. I asked her if she thought the war would ever end. She said, "I never imagined a nation could hate itself so much so early in its life." It wasn't really an answer. And I told her I didn't feel a part of "our nation" at all. "You'll be in Canada soon enough," she said. She sounded sad. I wonder if she doesn't want me to go. I want to ask her about her life outside of this house and if she has friends. But as far as I know, I'm the only person she ever talks to besides her husband and children. She's my entire world.

May 22, 1864

Tonight, the eldest boy, Randolph, came downstairs to

give me dinner and water. This was strange. I've come to look forward to my evening conversations with Mrs. Sheridan. I asked Randolph if his mother was all right. He said she was sick in bed. I pray she feels better soon.

May 23, 1864

Randolph again brought me lunch and dinner. He played with the baby for a little while, and I pestered him for information about his mother. But he doesn't know anything.

May 25, 1864

I still haven't seen Mrs. Sheridan. I hear footsteps overhead, making the floorboards creak. The footsteps are not the children's nor Mr. Sheridan's. They're unfamiliar. It can't be someone here to get me. It can't be. Then again, we haven't been careful lately. I've been at the table. I've been outside.

May 24, 1864 – Later

Mr. Sheridan just came downstairs. He looked weary and sweaty and under-slept. He handed me my dinner and sat quietly on the bed opposite until he got up the nerve to tell me what was going on. I stared at him without touching my food. I needed to know what was going on.

"She's got the fever," he explained.

I knew what he meant. The fever is Scarlet Fever. It's one of the deadliest. One year, it took out more than fifty slaves at the plantation. The fact that I was untouched has always made me feel both parts lucky and guilty. It was said I would never get it. That I was immune. But I know better than to believe everything doctors say.

I thought about telling Mr. Sheridan this but decided it wouldn't help.

"I have to send the children away for a while," he explained. "Just until she gets better."

The air between us stretched thin. I think we both know she won't get better. I can see it in Mr. Sheridan's eyes.

Now I sit alone in the darkness as Mary sleeps on. I'm thinking about Mrs. Sheridan upstairs—my only friend in the world—suffering. I want to go to her bedside. I want to tend to her. But there's no way to know if my "immunity" is real. I will not get sick. I will not leave my baby alone in this world.

May 31, 1864

The illness was not long. It took Mrs. Sheridan just as swiftly as it came. The house above me is empty and echo-ing, and nobody has brought me food in nearly twenty-four hours. I cannot blame them. I can only imagine what they have to deal with—burying a mother and a wife, sanitizing the house of the illness so that the children can return, putting on a brave face to the community, and all the while, maintaining the secrecy of my hiding place.

It was Mr. Sheridan who came downstairs to tell me. "She's gone." But he couldn't manage much more than that before hobbling back upstairs. I've been left to stew alone in my thoughts and ache with missing my friend.

The worst of it is my selfish fear that Mr. Sheridan will throw me out now that it's warm and he has so much to deal with here. I still haven't heard from Jane or Virgil. I fear that, even if they wrote a letter, the letter was lost in the chaos of the past few weeks. Maybe they think I'm dead by now. Maybe they think all is lost.

June 1, 1864

It was Randolph who brought me dinner tonight. I thanked him and cried for him.

June 3, 1864

I still do not know the state of my future. Mentally, I'm

preparing to leave again. I prepare for the fear of crossing that surging water and heading into the unknown. I am sure I will not survive.

It seems this godforsaken war will never end.

Chapter Nineteen

Wes couldn't believe how quickly The HISTORY Channel got to Martha's Vineyard. Within two weeks of Amanda's email to her friend, the entertainment lawyer, a camera crew was spread out across the front yard and street in front of the Sunrise Cove. Van doors were open, and sound, lighting, and camera equipment was everywhere—wires pointing all different directions, men adjusting beanies and removing things from black boxes. People in headphones were telling other people in headphones where to go and how quickly. Wes felt dropped into the hubbub of chaotic television. He could barely suppress his excitement.

Because Wes was a Sheridan and the one most closely related to Matthew and Wendy Sheridan, apparent members of the Underground Railroad, Wes was needed for an interview. What Sam had told Wes thus far about the history of the place made him feel discombobulated. He'd seen the photos of the runaway slaves who had once sought refuge in the basement and had learned of a diary

—one taken away for further inspection. But nobody knew what was in the diary yet. Wes felt haunted by it.

Quentin Copperfield was the tele-journalist for this particular HISTORY Channel documentary. Wes was flustered about meeting him, as he'd watched Quentin on the nightly news for decades before his abrupt departure last year. When Wes told him what a big fan he'd been, Quentin thanked him and said, "I'm so glad I can put my money and time into passion projects like this. When The HISTORY Channel reached out to me about an Underground Railroad site on Martha's Vineyard, I jumped on my sailboat and came over here immediately." Apparently, he lived on Nantucket these days. It made Wes smile even more.

A makeup artist approached Wes to put a layer of what felt like dust on his face.

"I'm ancient," Wes joked to the girl. "I don't think you can hide that."

"You look great," the makeup artist said. "I love the suit!"

Beatrice had helped Wes get dressed that morning in a tweed suit that made him look like a historian. He thanked her and turned as Quentin approached in a black suit and a pair of shiny shoes. He had a weird urge to call Anna and tell him that the "famous Quentin Copperfield" was here at the Sunrise Cove! But then he remembered that Quentin had never been famous when Anna was alive. She wouldn't have known about him at all.

The cameras were rolling, and the interview was set. Quentin led Wes on a walk around the Sunrise Cove and asked him about his extensive family history. Wes told him what he knew: that his grandparents had built the Sunrise Cove after a fire had destroyed another Victorian structure that had once been on this site and that it hadn't been an inn but rather a family home.

"And you never knew anything about the Underground Railroad site just downstairs?" Quentin asked. He stopped walking by the water, which allowed the camera to do a dramatic circle around them and show off the beautiful Sunrise Cove and the ocean.

"Nothing. I assume my grandparents didn't know about it," Wes said.

Just beyond the shot, many Sheridans had gathered for a picnic along the beach near the Sunrise Cove. They watched Wes expectantly. Amanda's face, in particular, alternated between nervousness and excitement. She was always so anxious. Wes wished he could take it away.

"We know a diary was discovered downstairs," Quentin said. "We're waiting for more information about its contents. Do you have any guesses?"

Wes laughed. "I can't even imagine. Maybe it's Wendy's. Perhaps she can give us some insight into what it meant to be alive during the Civil War."

"You're aware that Wendy died in 1864, correct?" Quentin said.

Wes faltered, and his smile dropped. Of course, he'd known that all of the Sheridans alive in the 1860s were long gone. But the fact that Wendy—the wife of Matthew and presumably one-half of their Underground Railroad team—had died so young startled him.

"I didn't know."

"She had Scarlet Fever," Quentin explained. "A few others on the island got it, too. We know because of some very old records that spoke of a brief yet deadly epidemic. The Sheridan children were sent elsewhere for a period of time until they knew it was safe. And all of the people who died of Scarlet Fever were buried in another part of the island, away from their loved ones."

Wes felt a pang of regret. He wrung out his hands. "I didn't know."

Quentin nodded, took his shoulder, and turned to look at the camera. "I think we'd better cut."

When the shot was over, Quentin's face transformed to show his worry.

"Wes, I'm so sorry for springing that on you," he said.

"It's okay." Wes shook his head. "It just caught me off guard. It's not like she ever really lived in the Sunrise Cove or was ever a part of my life in any way. Heck, I didn't even know her name till recently. But it's startling to think of so much pain. It must have affected my great-grandparents and even my grandparents in a way."

Quentin nodded. "Pain is always passed down. I truly believe that."

The crew decided to spend the rest of the afternoon getting exterior and interior shots of the Sunrise Cove and driving around the island for dramatic coastal scenes, views of tourists at the harbor, and shots of the light-houses. Quentin thanked Wes for his work so far, shook his hand, and retreated to meet the show's producer. This left Wes in the middle of the lawn between the Sunrise Cove and the Vineyard Sound, squeezing his hands into fists and looking up at the beautiful structure. The windows of the inn reminded him of eyes, peering at him.

"Grandpa!" Amanda called.

Wes turned to see Amanda, Audrey, and Susan waving him over. He put a bounce in his step as he approached and reminded himself to smile. This was all quite exciting. Sorrow about the past and Wendy's untimely death could be put to rest for now. A big spread of lunch options was set out across a blanket by the water, such as pulled pork, sliced watermelon, potato salad, four different types of cheeses, and three cakes: carrot, chocolate, and pineapple upside down. Amanda pulled a lawn chair out for him to sit.

"Thanks, Mandy," he said. "You know if I sit on the ground, I won't be able to get back up."

Amanda laughed and sat down on the blanket beside his lawn chair. Christine made him a plate with a little bit of everything and handed it over. With his fork poised, he realized everyone looked at him expectantly. They wanted to hear how the interview had gone.

"I didn't do too badly," he said with a laugh.

"You looked fantastic out there," Susan assured him.

"The suit is to die for," Audrey said.

Wes waved his fork as a blush crawled over his cheeks. "Quentin is an astonishingly intellectual man," he began.

Audrey leaned forward. Amanda nervously touched the baby carrier's edge, where Genevieve slept soundly.

"He mentioned something I didn't know," Wes declared. "Matthew's wife, Wendy Sheridan, died before the war ended. Scarlet Fever. 1864."

Susan furrowed her brow.

"Apparently, she's buried somewhere else on the island," Wes said. "They separated the sick from the normal cemetery. I can't say why learning that eats me up inside. I suppose there's just so little I know about my family that far back. And it's alarming to learn about the specifics of their pain."

Wes knew the specifics of his family's pain. He knew about Susan's first husband's affair and the breast cancer that had nearly taken her from them. He knew about

Christine's longtime anger and her lack of stability and her loss of an ovary. He knew about Lola's wayward nature that so often masked her real fear of sitting still for too long and facing herself. And he knew about his own pain—the loss of Anna, the loss of his memory, his fear that he was already losing the future before he'd reached it.

So many generations of Sheridans had been born and died on this island. *It was a privilege to be one of them,* Wes thought. But as he sat with his family in contemplative silence, his heart felt bruised. He wasn't ready to leave Martha's Vineyard yet. His story wasn't yet over. Had Wendy felt the same way?

Chapter Twenty

Grandpa Wes was quiet for the rest of the picnic. Amanda and Audrey made eye contact several times, stewing with questions about what to do and how to cheer him up. In the distance, the camera crew encircled the inn to get shots from every angle, then set up the camera to take shots of the family spread out across the grass, picnicking. Amanda could already imagine Quentin's voice-over: "In 2024, nearly two hundred years after their ancestors hid ex-slaves on their quest for freedom, the Sheridan family is bigger and closer than ever."

Eventually, Amanda's mother packed up her bag and admitted she had to head back to the office because playtime was over. One after another, the other Sheridans did the same: curling up the tops of chip bags and piling the pulled pork into Tupperware containers. Genevieve got fussy, so Amanda wrapped her against her chest and strolled along the water's edge barefoot so that the grass curled between her toes. When she turned, she watched as Audrey picked up Max and put him against her hip while Noah loaded the Tupperware containers in his arms. Sam was far in the distance, talking to Quentin Copperfield and one of the producers about filming schedules. The amount the producers had agreed to pay to film at the Sunrise Cove Inn would at least get them through the summer. That was one obstacle cleared.

Sam said that the publicity from The HISTORY Channel would probably bring in heaps of tourists after it aired. Amanda wasn't sure when that would be. Editing took a little while, didn't it? Television schedules were almost as tricky as baby schedules.

Before Amanda turned away, she was surprised to see Cynthia walk around the side of the van. She wore a smart pair of tailored pants, a tank top, and a blazer with shoulder pads straight out of the eighties. She made it work without question—a fashionable skill she'd had since Amanda met her years ago.

It startled Amanda yet again that it wasn't so long ago when they'd met. Becoming a mother had put everything back then into the "before" category.

"Amanda!" Cynthia called, waving her hand.

"What are you doing here?" Amanda called back, hurrying toward her gently so as not to wake Genevieve.

"Look at you!" Cynthia cried as she got closer. "You're a portrait of health and womanhood. That baby is gorgeous. And so are you!"

Amanda laughed. "I've hardly slept more than two hours at a time since she was born. I feel ragged."

"You look like a dream. But you always did," Cynthia said, giving Amanda a side hug so as not to disturb the baby. "This place is stunning, Amanda. I can't believe you held out on me during law school. Not that I took much time away from studying to visit beautiful places." Cynthia sighed.

"It all worked out for you, though," Amanda pointed out. "You're in the big leagues."

"And you!" Cynthia said. "You're working alongside your mother, right? The great Susan Sheridan, one of the best who ever did it. I think I read about one of the cases you took on last year. A very rich family…" She touched her ear in thought.

Amanda groaned.

"What's up?" Cynthia's eyes widened.

"You're thinking of the Arnouts," Amanda said.

"That's right! That rich playboy kid who destroyed the dean of Harvard's house. And hurt his girlfriend? That was such a wild story. Like, who did he think he was?"

Amanda's head pounded at the memory. She tried to laugh it off, but it sounded strained.

"I didn't win that case," Amanda said finally.

"Who could have won that case? He was caught red-handed. Literally." Cynthia was still smiling. She understood the legal world far more than nearly anyone in Amanda's life, save for her mother. Maybe she could handle the truth of Amanda's current predicament.

"As I remember it, you got his sentence down to basically nothing," Cynthia said.

"Just a year," Amanda said, allowing herself a moment of pride. It truly had been sensational proof that she knew what she was doing in the legal world. But it had all crumbled at her feet.

Cynthia studied her face for a moment as Amanda stewed in shame. Her mind's eye filled with the last moments of the trial of when the judge had announced the jury's decision; when Hilton Arnout had turned his greedy blue eyes to Amanda and sized her up in a way that made her feel as though he planned to eat her alive. She wondered who he was making miserable in that low-security prison he was in. Who he controlled with his parents' money and his narcissism.

Cynthia touched Amanda's arm tenderly. "What's up? Are you good? Do you want to get a cup of coffee or something?"

Amanda glanced back at her family. Most everyone was packed up and continuing along with their days. Even Audrey had moved on, waving back to Amanda as she hurried Max elsewhere. He was in the midst of one of his classic toddler tantrums, and Audrey was frantic, cheeks red.

Amanda was faced with the weight of her afternoon. Hours alone at home with her baby, feeling somewhere between dreams and nightmares, nursing her, rocking her, attempting to feed herself until it all happened again. Cynthia looked at her the way she'd once been looked at —as though she were just another lawyer with a big head of knowledge resting atop her shoulders.

She'd always known it objectively but couldn't have understood it until she experienced it. Mothers often lost their sense of self. They became bodies first. They were needed physically. It was exhausting.

"Sure. A coffee sounds great," Amanda said. She couldn't resist a bit of intellectual stimulation, even if she regretted it later.

One of the producers marched past and asked to talk to Cynthia for a moment about a contractual problem with another client. Amanda watched as Cynthia transformed immediately into her lawyer self, using language that hadn't come out of Amanda's mouth since the birth of Genevieve. When Cynthia returned to Amanda's side, she grunted, "Maybe I'll need something a little stronger than that coffee."

Amanda laughed. "I know a good place."

Instead of the coffee shop down the road, Amanda led Cynthia to her favorite natural wine bar near the harbor. Her nursing schedule rarely allowed her a glass of wine, but she'd pumped enough milk to give herself a window. Cynthia was terrifically excited. Her eyes reminded Amanda of a golden retriever's as she scanned the gorgeous water and the bobbing sailboats. She nodded tentatively and said, "I think I just saw Ryan Reynolds?"

Amanda raised her shoulders. Celebrities could always be spotted in Martha's Vineyard. Wasn't Cynthia used to that out in Los Angeles?

Amanda ordered a glass of orange wine; Cynthia went for rose and a plate of cheeses with crackers, fresh bread, and olives. Amanda could have eaten all of it herself and ordered a second, but she held herself back and raised her glass of wine.

"To being back together again," Cynthia said.

"Cheers to that."

Amanda filled her mouth with orange wine and suppressed a groan. Was this the best thing she'd tasted in ages? It was certainly better than the microwavable dinner she'd made herself last night. (If Audrey had seen her, she never would have let her forget about it.)

Cynthia tapped the tips of her fingers against the tabletop. "Brett, the producer, is over the moon about this stop. He loves the Sunrise Cove. Says it's exactly what his viewership is into. Quaint small-town America merges with the historical Underground Railroad. It really hits a sweet spot."

Amanda had known it would that day she'd reached out to Cynthia.

"You have a great eye for this sort of thing," Cynthia said.

"I got lucky. This is my family's inn." Amanda shrugged. "It just fell into my lap."

Cynthia laughed. "Not everyone would have understood how to capitalize on something like that. I understand that the inn had to close down?"

Amanda cringed and filled her mouth with wine.

"Amanda, what's up? You look pale as a ghost. Should I order you more food?" Cynthia's eyes echoed compassion.

Amanda was wordless. How could she explain everything? How could she be so laissez-faire?

"I know we haven't seen each other in a few years, but we're friends, Amanda. At least, I like to think we are," Cynthia said. Her palms were flat on the table, and she looked at Amanda with eyes prepared to bore holes into her to make sense of this.

Genevieve remained asleep on her chest. Amanda took a deep breath, unsure of what would come out of her mouth when she spoke.

"I'm sorry I'm acting so strange. The baby has been a lot, obviously. But more than that..." Amanda trailed off. "That trial you mentioned. Hilton Arnout?"

"Hilton! That was his name. He was crazy handsome, right? He looked like an advertisement for Wilson tennis balls."

Amanda grimaced. "His parents are very unhappy with his guilty verdict."

"That's rich parents," Cynthia said with a shrug. "You explained how lucky he was to get just a year, right?"

"I did, yeah. But they don't believe me. They think I failed their son."

"That's stupid." Cynthia put a square of cheese in her mouth and chewed, as though this were the easiest thing in the world. "It's wild how stupid rich people can be sometimes. But in Hollywood, I work with some pretty empty-headed actors. And producers. And set designers." She scratched her ear. "And directors, now that I think about it. Most everyone is pretty helpless."

Amanda stifled a laugh. Cynthia's performance—if it was a performance—was comical and gorgeous. It took her back to college.

"Big deal," Cynthia said. "They can have their pity party and move on."

"It isn't that simple," Amanda said. Her eyes pricked with tears. "The Arnouts know people in Massachusetts. The governor and all of the governor's friends are in their pockets. And they made a few phone calls to get my license suspended."

Cynthia's jaw dropped. "What?"

Amanda raised her shoulders. Just saying this aloud, just being heard, loosened the knots in her chest.

Cynthia put down her glass of wine. "I mean, how is that even possible?"

"Money is old out here," Amanda said. "Family names go a long way."

"This is ridiculous." Cynthia's cheeks were tomato red. "I work in one of the most narcissistic and nepotism-based businesses in the world, if not the most. I've heard of people attempting to do something this heinous, but I've never heard of anyone succeeding."

"The Arnouts are capable of anything."

Cynthia's hand shot into her purse. She hunted around until she found her cell and dialed someone without saying another word. Amanda's heart seized. Cynthia's eyes had hardened to tiny blue ice cubes.

"Georgia? It's Cynthia. Yeah, I'm out East." Cynthia's tone was authoritative. "Can you set up a call with Baxter for tomorrow morning? Tell him it's urgent." Cynthia clucked her tongue and fidgeted with her fork. "Nine a.m. your time, noon my time. Perfect. Looking forward." She then stamped the phone on the table, picked up an olive, and plopped it into her mouth as though that was that.

Amanda stuttered. "Who is Baxter?"

"Baxter is one of the most powerful lawyers I know in the entire state of California," Cynthia explained. "He started out in criminal law before transferring to entertainment law. He wanted to live in Los Angeles, and he wanted to make buckets of cash. That's the way."

Amanda peered at Cynthia. Her head pounded with confusion.

"Baxter knows people, too," Cynthia explained. "I see no reason he can't make a few phone calls and get this monkey off your back. He owes me a favor."

Amanda couldn't believe it. Was Cynthia her fairy godmother, come to transform her pumpkin into a carriage and her rags into a ballroom gown?

"Seriously, these rich people love to swing their weight around," Cynthia said sternly, "but they can't get away with this. This is America. We have laws for a reason. And we're lawyers, Amanda. We have to use those same laws to protect ourselves and each other." Cynthia picked up another slice of cheese and put it on her tongue. "Now, let's talk about something more interesting, shall we? Tell me how you met your husband. Last I knew, you were dating that horrible guy. What was his name? Chris? Just awful." Her eyes shone. She wanted to gossip like old friends.

Amanda's heart had begun to beat again. She matched Cynthia's grin. "It turns out Chris was just as awful as you say. Why didn't you tell me?"

Cynthia cackled. "He's nowhere near as cute as your husband either."

"My mother hired him to be the manager at the Sunrise Cove," Amanda said. "As you know, I moved back here after…" She remembered herself at her first wedding and Chris's abandonment. "After my life flipped upside down. But Sam was right there in front of me. Laughing with me. Always remembering little details about me. My heart was so bruised, and I told myself I didn't have space in it to fall in love again."

"We don't always have a choice about when we fall in love, do we?" Cynthia said with a sigh.

"Are you in love?" Amanda asked.

"Me? No way," Cynthia said. "I'm in love with my career and myself right now. I'm dating all over Los Angeles, of course. Mostly very attractive actors." Her eyes sparkled. "But they're all pretty egotistical and eager to use my connections to better their careers. I almost always kick them to the curb."

"Almost?" Amanda laughed.

"If they have stellar talent or a killer jawline, I send them along to my friend who works as an agent," Cynthia explained. "No use letting them go to waste!"

Amanda was fascinated with Cynthia. For a little while, they'd had similar lives, gone to the same school, and even lived just a few blocks away from one another.

But now, Cynthia's life had transformed to Technicolor Los Angeles highways and long Californian beaches and high-end designer wear. Amanda's life was diapers and sleepless nights and flicking through television channels as her brain turned to goop.

But Cynthia had promised that she could get Amanda's career back up and running with her connections. The Arnouts couldn't touch her.

Chapter Twenty-One

Wes returned to the Sunrise Cove every morning that week to meet with Quentin and watch the television crew. They didn't always need him, but Wes liked to be close to the action—listening to Quentin talk about the Sheridan family, interviewing the on-site historians, and showing off artifacts such as the photographs Matthew had taken and kept downstairs. Wes felt drawn deeper into the world of Matthew and Wendy, into their fears regarding the Underground Railroad and their family's safety. So immersed was he in the past that he nearly forgot his Wednesday afternoon meeting with Dr. Hamilton to go over the results of his tests.

Wes tore through the doctor's office door at ten past his appointment time. The receptionist greeted him happily and said, "We were just about to call Beatrice to see if you were with her." Wes staggered to a halt and blinked at her. He had to bite his tongue from saying, *No. I don't want to tell Beatrice about this drug. I don't want her to know that I've gotten so much worse.*

He wanted to start taking the drug without her knowledge and immediately transform into a healthier and happier individual. He wanted it to seem like magic.

Dr. Hamilton studied a clipboard as Wes entered the office and sat down. Wes wondered if Dr. Hamilton was looking at his results again. Perhaps he was preparing himself to tell Wes just how bad the situation was. That the future was bleaker than he'd realized. That his memory would soon be only scraps.

Instead, he said, "We just have one more test for you before I feel fully ready to get you started on the medication."

Wes straightened his spine.

"I know I said that last time," Dr. Hamilton said, "but we have to be one hundred percent sure. Is that all right?"

Wes could wait a little bit longer if it meant getting approved. He smiled. "Thanks for taking such good care of me, Doc."

"Thanks for taking such good care of yourself!" Dr. Hamilton said. "It's every doctor's dream."

Wes left the doctor's office with a skip to his step and returned to his home with Beatrice to make a turkey sandwich and sit outside. It was a clear-blue-sky day. Sparrows tittered across the sky and played, reminding Wes of the spunkiness of nature. Nothing ever took itself so seriously. And he shouldn't, either.

Beatrice texted that she was out with a few friends and would be home after dinner. "There's frozen lasagna in the freezer," she said. "Just heat it up in the microwave if you want. Love you!"

Wes made a mug of tea and wrote a few things down in his ledger, including what the historian had told him over coffee that morning, that he wanted to create a photography exhibition for Matthew Sheridan's photos of ex-slaves. He envisioned it in Manhattan of all places. Wes ached with excitement. He imagined himself in Manhattan as a representative for Matthew Sheridan. He imagined his sister Kerry beside him—the eldest Sheridan. When Wes had asked Kerry if she wanted to be featured on The HISTORY Channel, she'd wrinkled her nose and said, "Nobody wants to see an old lady on screen." That wasn't true, of course. The truth was that Kerry was camera shy. She had no interest in fame. She was happy as she was.

A knock on the front door took Wes out of his reverie. He walked to the foyer and opened it to find Quentin Copperfield. His eyes were rimmed with red. Wes's immediate fear was that the show would be canceled, and they would have to return the money.

"Quentin, this is a surprise."

"I hope you don't mind me coming over like this," Quentin said. "We tried your cell, but you didn't pick up."

Wes had turned off the sound on his phone so as not to annoy the birds.

"Come in!" Wes said. He glanced around as he led Quentin into the house and through the kitchen, cursing that he'd left out the plate from his sandwich. He didn't want Quentin Copperfield to think he was a slob. "Sorry about the mess."

Quentin waved his hand. "It looks fantastic. Really." He sounded like he meant it. "Do you have a place to sit down? I want to tell you something. The network wanted me to spring it on you on-camera and surprise you again, but I couldn't bring myself to do it. It feels too cruel."

Wes's heart dropped into his stomach. What on earth was this about? Quentin had already revealed the untimely death of Wendy Sheridan. He wasn't sure he could take much more in terms of long-ago deaths and family secrets.

Wes led Quentin to the back porch and sat down across from him. Perhaps he should have gotten him a cup of tea? But it seemed trivial when compared to the aching look in Quentin's eyes. Quentin folded his hands on the table and looked ahead. It made him look just as he had at his nightly news desk when he was about to give the day's news to America. Wes took a breath.

"We've received word from the historian up in Boston. The one with the diary," Quentin said.

Wes's hands were clammy.

"It looks like the diary was written by an ex-slave named Martha," Quentin said. "She took refuge in the basement, where she gave birth to a baby. The baby was very sick, and she stayed with the Sheridans while her husband and sister went north. It seems that the Sheridans and Martha struck a wonderful bond. They even brought her upstairs sometimes for real meals and to go outside to see the stars and breathe fresh air."

Wes's throat was very tight. He clenched his hands into fists to try to keep himself from crying.

"As we discussed that first time, Wendy died of Scarlet Fever in 1864. Martha was terrified she'd have to leave after that. But Matthew kept her in the basement until after the war, when she moved upstairs and took on a role as a sort of live-in maid and nanny. By that time, her baby was a year and a half old, and the Sheridan children were between the ages of two and eight. There was a great deal to do."

"Wow. So she really stayed on Martha's Vineyard!" Wes said happily. He was pleased as punch that she'd been allowed this second chance of life on his island, with his family.

Quentin folded his lips. "There's more to this story. The diary indicates that Martha became pregnant again in 1867. That was two years after the war ended."

Wes's jaw went slack. Quentin's eyes were filled with questions.

"It doesn't say who the father was?" Wes asked.

Quentin shook his head. "No. Martha explains she's pregnant, and the diary ends shortly after that."

Wes's heart pounded. "Did she die?"

"We don't know," Quentin said. "It's certainly possible. As forward-thinking as the North was back then, they weren't so forward-thinking as to keep wonderful records regarding ex-slaves. If Martha did die—either due to pregnancy or another illness, it's unlikely that Matthew lingered on the event for very long. He would have had five children in his house. Or four, if he sent Martha's daughter off to live elsewhere. That isn't recorded anywhere that we've discovered yet, either."

Wes wrinkled his forehead. He couldn't imagine this; he couldn't fathom what would bring someone to throw a very young child out of the house. He wanted to insist that Matthew had raised Martha's child as his own. But he also knew how naive that thought truly was. Times were far different in 1867 than in 2024. Racial tension was still high in America to this day. It was unfathomable to think back that far.

Wes cleared his throat. "Is it possible that Matthew was the father of Martha's second baby?"

Quentin didn't flinch. "It certainly is the most likely case."

Wes thought that, too.

"But something like that wouldn't have played well in the community at that time," Quentin explained. "If they learned Martha was pregnant by Matthew, it's possible they turned their backs on the Sheridan family." He cleared his throat. "Is there any mention of that in family lore? A story about the Sherians needing to work their way back to good social standing on the Vineyard?"

Wes racked his mind for answers. Again, he pictured his grandmother hovering above him, combing his hair and telling him stories. None of them were applicable.

"I don't think so," Wes said. "I certainly don't know any."

Quentin placed his hands on his thighs and turned to gaze out across the water. Wes wondered if they were both thinking the same thoughts about imagining a poor ex-slave woman who'd found refuge in the Sheridan House—only for everything to go awry just a couple of years later. What had happened? Where had her child wound up? And was it possible to ever peel back the layers of history to learn the truth?

Quentin left a few minutes later. He gave Wes a firm handshake on his way out the door and said, "If you think of anything, give me a call." He also said they had an entire team of historians up in Boston poring over the diary, looking for more clues about Martha and what might have happened to her. "We won't leave a stone unturned," he promised.

Wes sat on the back porch until the temperature plummeted and rain splattered across the windowpanes. Shivering, he went inside to heat more water and put on a big fuzzy sweater, a gift from Susan last Christmas. As the water kettle roared, the front door opened, and he listened as Beatrice performed all the duties after her short walk through the rain, such as removing her coat and shaking it out, coughing out the chill in her lungs, and putting her shoes by the door.

"Wes?" Beatrice called.

Wes felt achy and very old. "I'm just in here," he said. He poured the hot water into a cup and tried to smile as Beatrice entered.

Beatrice's face fell when she saw him. "What's wrong?"

How could Wes fully translate the brevity of his emotions? How could he say that one woman's diary and lost future had reminded him of his own memories that slipped through his fingers? How could he explain his fear that Matthew Sheridan hadn't been as tremendously kind and good as someone in 2024 might have been—only because of the nature of time and public opinion?

Wes explained what he knew about the diary, about Martha, about her first baby and what they knew of her second pregnancy. He half expected Beatrice to say something like, *I know it's upsetting, Wes, but this has nothing to do with you. It all happened almost two hundred years ago!*

Beatrice wrapped her arms around him and held him as he swayed. A few minutes later, they abandoned his tea on the counter and retreated to the bedroom, where they dressed in pajamas and lay in the warmth of each other's bodies. The rain had intensified, and Wes felt cocooned. Eventually, he drifted off to sleep.

But later that night, he again found himself out by the water, drenched to the bone. He'd sleepwalked to the edge of the shore as though he was hunting for something in his dreams. He put his hand over his mouth to keep himself from screaming with panic and frustration. If the new medication didn't come through, he would have to make peace with locked doors. He wouldn't be able to trust himself again.

Chapter Twenty-Two

Nobody could have anticipated the mess that came with Cynthia's call with Baxter, the entertainment lawyer. Cynthia had called Amanda to say, "Baxter's on the case! It should be over soon." Amanda had floated through the rest of the afternoon like a flower petal on a breeze. As originally planned, she would return to work when Genevieve was three months old. This would be just a hiccup. A brief reminder that she couldn't let anyone "powerful" make her afraid.

But by that evening, everything changed again. Susan appeared at the front door of Amanda and Sam's house. Her face was the color of marshmallow. "I need to talk to you," she said as she entered and tugged her hair into a high ponytail.

Susan sat at the kitchen table as Amanda remained standing so that she could bob around and put Genevieve back to sleep. The scene was comical with a clown and a lawyer in the kitchen.

"We have to go to court," Susan said.

Amanda's heart thumped. She had a hunch who was behind this, but she didn't want to believe it.

Susan's eyes flickered. "They're going after the entire agency now. They could take away my license and Bruce's."

Amanda's jaw dropped. "No!"

"They said something about us 'escalating the issue and dragging their name,'" Susan said.

Amanda swallowed, remembering Cynthia's call. "My friend tried to fix this," she said. "She knows people who know people…"

Susan rubbed her eyes and brought away her fingers, which were covered with black eyeliner. "Oh."

Amanda's stomach tied into knots. But this wasn't her fault, she reminded herself. And it wasn't Cynthia's either.

"It doesn't matter." Susan sighed. "We're going to fight them, and we're going to win. I don't know a single judge who would look at our case and rule in favor of the Arnouts."

But Amanda wasn't so sure. "They've already done so much damage. What makes you think they don't have all the judges around here in their pocket, too?"

Susan's chin quivered. Amanda considered throwing her career under the bus in order to save her mother's. Amanda was still young. She could still find something else to do. Something to hang her life's meaning upon. Probably.

"Let's take it one day at a time," Susan suggested. She eyed Genevieve and softened. "Do you feel up to heading to court mid-June? Bruce and I are throwing ourselves into the case, but we need you to be involved. You'll need to make a statement. I might even want you up on the stand."

"I'll do anything," Amanda said. Mid-June was still about a month away. Genevieve would grow and change exponentially by then. Summer would nearly unfurl.

Chapter Twenty-Three

The day The HISTORY Channel wrapped filming at the Sunrise Cove, Wes and Quentin shared a final hug and promised to visit one another soon. "Us Copperfields are just an island away," Quentin said as he got into the producer's car to be taken to his boat in the harbor. Wes raised a hand as they drove away and disappeared on the other side of the ice creamery and gift shop.

Wes stood alone on the front lawn of the Sunrise Cove and peered up at the windows. They were dark and latched tight, still waiting for the next generation of guests to transform the inn to its former glory. The historian on-duty had said he still wasn't sure when they could re-open. He supposed he would get the all clear soon, especially now that the basement room had been analyzed down to the finest detail and the diary had been assessed. The historians had met with Sam last night to discuss how they should proceed from a museum standpoint. They wanted to make it a historical site on Martha's Vineyard and allow guests to enter and pay ticket prices. But would the Sunrise Cove see that revenue? Sam said he wasn't sure.

But Wes couldn't care less, right now, about the state of the Sunrise Cove's cashflow. That weight sat squarely on Sam's shoulders.

Wes's phone vibrated in his pocket, and he pulled it out to answer. It was Beatrice. His heart surged.

"Hey! You finished up over there?" Beatrice asked.

"Just about," Wes said.

"I just ran into Susan. Kellan came home to surprise his dad for his birthday. We're invited for dinner."

Wes smiled. It had been ages since he'd seen Kellan— a once-troubled-teenager who'd grown into a remarkable young man.

"I can practically see you smile over the phone," Beatrice teased. "I'll swing by the Sunrise Cove and pick you up. We have to bring a bottle of wine."

Beatrice appeared in front of the inn a few minutes later. She had the windows of her BMW convertible cracked, and a breeze swept through her silver curls. She stopped just long enough for Wes to swagger around the front of the car (in his mind, he swaggered, though it probably looked more like a waddle) and get in. He kissed her on the cheek and the lips, and she giggled and swatted him away.

"The traffic is incredible," she said. "I want to get out of here."

After a brief stop at her favorite wine store, they drove the rest of the way to Susan's place. Susan and Scott lived next door to the old Sheridan House. Sometimes Wes still panged with regret for having left that side of the beach. As he got out of the car, he turned as Audrey and Max crept through the woods that separated Susan's from the

Sheridan House, and Max squealed with laughter and ran toward Wes. It was truly remarkable that Max would grow up in the Sheridan House. It was the only home he'd ever known.

They found Susan and Scott hard at work in the kitchen. They were making steaks and salad. Susan hurried to throw her arms around Wes and usher him toward the porch, where Kellan, Amanda, Sam, and Noah waited on everyone else.

"I don't get it," Noah was saying as Wes entered. "You're going to court with the parents of the guy you just represented?"

Amanda grimaced and took a sip of her wine. She forcefully changed her face when she saw Wes, Beatrice, Audrey, and Max and shot Noah a look that told him the conversation was over. "Hi, Grandpa!"

"Don't switch the topic on my account," Wes said.

"It's boring," Amanda insisted.

"It's not! These rich idiots think they can walk all over Amanda and Aunt Susie," Audrey said, scowling as she adjusted Max in a chair and gave him a granola bar.

Wes tilted his head. Beatrice grabbed a seat at the end of the table as Kellan bolted up the back steps and back onto the porch. For a moment, Wes took stock of him—long-legged, taller than he'd been at Christmas, with a tan face and shoulders that spoke of hours outside. Had Scott said something about Kellan taking a job outdoors? Or was this from birdwatching?

"Grandpa," Kellan said as he shot forward to hug him. "It's so good to see you."

Wes panged with love for the kid. As their hug broke, Kellan rifled through a bag of chips and sat down, gesturing for Wes to sit beside him. Wes felt lucky. The guest of honor wanted Wes, of all people, to sit with him.

"When did all this happen again?" Audrey demanded of Amanda.

Wes blinked from Audrey to Amanda. His brain felt foggy and inarticulate. What were they talking about again?

"Let's just drop it, okay?" Amanda said. Her cheeks were pink, the way they got when she was embarrassed.

"Don't switch the topic on my account," Wes said.

The mood at the table stalled. Amanda gave him a worried look and sucked in her cheeks. Wes's heart banged in his chest. Had he said something wrong? He turned to look at Beatrice, feeling like a man drowning in a swimming pool.

A few seconds later, Noah brought up a game of base-ball he and Sam had caught on television, and Kellan chimed in that he'd seen it, too. Wes's hands were sweaty, and he felt as though his clothes didn't fit. He stood abruptly and wandered to the edge of the porch so he could catch sight of the front porch of the Sheridan House next door. He took a step, then another down the porch steps, wondering if he could just walk through the line of trees and rejoin his old life. Why wasn't it that simple?

A hand touched his shoulder. Wes turned to find Beatrice gazing down at him from the top step. "Let's take a quick walk before dinner," she said.

Wes wanted to protest, but something in Beatrice's eyes made him understand that she meant business. He shrugged.

Beatrice and Wes walked to the water. Beatrice took

his hand and stuttered over her introduction. "I need to tell you something."

But Wes was still thinking about the incident on the back porch. "Did I say something wrong?"

"You just repeated yourself," Beatrice said kindly. "It could have happened to anyone."

Wes felt a jolt of recognition. When he'd repeated himself—so soon after the fact—it only confirmed his dementia diagnosis. He'd freaked everyone out.

Beatrice didn't look frightened, though. She adjusted her fingers so that they were laced all the way through his and said, "I talked to Dr. Hamilton today."

Wes's heart skipped a beat. "Oh."

Beatrice's eyes gleamed, as though she were holding in tears. "The reason I called him was because I'd read about a new 'miracle' drug for dementia patients. I didn't want to get my hopes up about it. I just wanted to ask him if he'd heard about it and if he had any information." Beatrice squeezed Wes's hand harder. "He was surprised you hadn't told me about it. He said you've been under-going tests to see if you're a candidate."

Wes felt squeamish. "I didn't forget to tell you," he said. "I just wasn't sure I wanted to. I didn't want to get your hopes up either." He sighed. "Those nightmares scare me, Beatrice. I know they're an indication that everything is getting worse. And the fact that it's all coming right before the wedding? It's terrible timing."

Beatrice was quiet. Wes half imagined her calling off the wedding right here and now. *If you're not well enough to be with me, then it has to be over.*

But instead, she said, "I'm just so pleased you're already on the path to getting that medication!" She looked ten years younger. She threw her arms around

Wes and let out a single sob. When their hug broke, she said in a flurry of words, "I read numerous studies about it. I read testimonials. I even watched a two-hour documentary about a woman whose life was completely changed by this drug." She shook her head. "The fact that you might be just a week or two away from taking it floors me. More than that, the fact that you've had the wherewithal to do this all yourself proves that you're much healthier, still, than you think you are."

Wes tried to melt in her flattery. He tucked one of her curls behind her ear and imagined them at the altar pledging the rest of their lives to one another in a few weeks. He imagined that his brain would be firing on all cylinders by then. That Beatrice would be proud to call him her husband.

But there were no guarantees in this life. When Wes and Beatrice were called back to the porch table for steak, Wes clutched Beatrice's hand under the table and listened to his remarkable family joke and laugh and tease one another. He cackled as Amanda told a story about baby Genevieve—who would soon be six weeks old. The sun dropped into the Vineyard Sound and cast the island in fiery oranges and pinks and reds. And just before the light died out altogether, Wes spotted a stork flying out across the water, its wingspan at least four feet. It was incredible.

Chapter Twenty-Four

The court date was set for June 13, 2024. Amanda watched the date approach on her calendar as her anxiety spiked and her baby grew a nice and healthy belly and a funny little personality. Amanda's moods were all over the place, but she tried never to show them to Genevieve. There was no telling what a little baby could remember; no telling how your actions shifted into their view of the world. One of her newer recurring nightmares involved an adult Genevieve telling her future partner, *"My mother was always so angry."*

Two nights before the court date—to be held at Nantucket Courthouse—Amanda was in the living room with Sam, sharing a bottle of wine and unwinding after a long day of preparation. Sam told her that the historians were pretty sure they were "close to cracking the case of what happened to Martha," and Amanda was fascinated. Martha was the ex-slave who'd kept the diary. Apparently, she'd learned to read and write from the women she'd worked for in Georgia. Throughout the diary, she championed the fact that her daughter would know how to read and write from childhood. She would have a completely different sort of life than the people Martha had grown up around. And didn't every mother want their babies to have more than they had?

"We have to assume that Matthew was the second baby's father, right?" Amanda said, sitting cross-legged on the couch.

"I don't know. Peering that far back through history is like trying to see to the bottom of the ocean," Sam said.

Amanda rubbed her temples. She imagined Martha's romantic life on the island during the few years after the war. Perhaps she'd met someone at a market, a handsome fisherman or a farmer. Maybe there had been other Black people on Martha's Vineyard—ex-slaves or otherwise. Perhaps they had a community that Amanda knew nothing about.

When she said this to Sam, Sam shrugged.

"If she really met someone else, maybe she went away with him," Sam suggested. "She took her first baby and left the Sheridans behind."

Amanda decided she liked this storyline the best. "I'm just so happy she got out of that basement," she said, shivering.

Sam had told her that the only reason Martha had been able to breathe down there was because Matthew Sheridan had built a vent system that allowed air inside. But that meant the basement room had probably been awfully frigid during the winter.

The baby monitor blared with Genevieve's anger. Sam hopped up to go tend to her, assuring Amanda it was all right and he would take care of it. Amanda topped off her wine and listened intently, waiting for Genevieve to calm down. She wasn't as accustomed to her father, but he normally did the trick. Amanda's mother had told her that Richard had never been so keen to help out with their babies. That he'd left Susan to weather the chaos alone.

But Sam and Richard were practically night and day.

But Genevieve wasn't calming down this time. After two full minutes of continuous howling, Amanda hopped to her feet to save poor Sam.

Sam was in the rocking chair with Genevieve in his arms. Genevieve's face was bright red, and she kicked her legs and punched her fists angrily. She had the strength of a boxer.

"I think there's something wrong," Sam said.

Amanda dropped to her knees to take Genevieve. The baby's skin was scalding hot. Amanda nearly screeched with surprise. "Oh, baby," she breathed, bringing Genevieve to her chest. "Can you get the thermometer, Sam?"

Sam stalled for a moment, gaping at them. Amanda glared at him—something she would regret later, and he jumped up to get the thermometer and come back. She didn't want to be the sort of woman who showed anger in stressful situations. She had to be calm and forward-thinking, like Susan.

Genevieve hadn't been sick since birth. She was nearly two months old, a portrait of baby happiness and health. Where on earth had she picked up this germ? The grocery store? Audrey? Max? Amanda's thoughts twisted into knots as she searched for someone or something to blame. When Sam appeared, she nearly wept along with Genevieve.

The thermometer read 102.5 Fahrenheit.

"We have to go to the hospital," Amanda said. She

sounded exactly like her mother. Authoritative. The sort of woman who knew what needed to be done.

Sam flew around the nursery to prepare. Amanda carried Genevieve downstairs and told herself to remain calm. If she panicked, Genevieve would sense it and probably get frightened. She needed to operate this as though it were any other day.

Somewhere in the dark recesses of Amanda's mind, she was fully freaking out. She would deal with that later. She would cry when she was alone.

Sam nearly hit Amanda's car when he backed out of the driveway. Amanda yelped just in the nick of time, then got in the back seat to put Genevieve in her car seat. All the way to the hospital, Sam and Amanda spoke in circles and never really said anything at all. They talked about their health insurance, about the doctors they knew up at the hospital, and about other babies they'd known who'd had fevers. But they felt on the brink of disaster.

Amanda thought to herself, *terrible things happen all the time. But please, don't let them happen now. Not here. Not to my baby.*

For whatever reason, as Amanda unbuckled the car seat and carried Genevieve into the hospital, she thought back to that long-ago day when Chris had left her at the altar. She'd thought to herself, then, *this is the worst day of my life.* But she'd been so naive.

It was a slow night at the emergency room. A nurse brought them to their own room down the hall in the children's wing and told them to relax because a doctor was on his way. It was nine thirty at night, and out the window, they could see the lighthouse beaming in the distance. Amanda had read that none of the lighthouses in America required any human involvement at all anymore. It saddened her. It seemed like there should have always been someone to keep watch.

Doctors and nurses buzzed in and out of their hospital room for several hours. Genevieve looked so tiny and helpless in her little white crib. They put a hospital bracelet around her little wrist and spoke to one another in soft yet authoritative voices, moving Amanda and Sam to the side when they needed to check on her. Not long after they arrived, they decided she was too dehydrated and inserted a tube that would help both with that and with sleep. Amanda's face was wet with tears. It felt like a horror film. Amanda kept thinking she would wake up in bed, the sheets twisted between her legs. But the night just kept going.

Genevieve's fever dipped to 101.4 at three that morning. This was still remarkably high for such a young baby but more manageable. Sam promptly sat on a plastic chair and fell asleep, his head lolling to the side. But Amanda felt as though her skin didn't fit her body. She remained at Genevieve's bedside and watched her sleep, making small deals with herself as a way to ensure Genevieve got well again. *I'll never curse. I'll never do anything wrong. I'll represent only the kindest criminals. I'll switch careers.* It was a never-ending stream of nonsensical thoughts.

Sam woke up with a start at seven when the doctor arrived to check on Genevieve again. Her fever remained high—101.2. Amanda's legs were like quivering reeds. Sam excused himself for the bathroom and returned with two cups of coffee. He rubbed his eyes and hugged Amanda from behind, kissing the back of her neck as they gazed at their baby. When Max spent many weeks in the NICU, Amanda couldn't have comprehended Audrey's terror. She was getting closer to understanding.

Amanda didn't think to call her mother to let her know she couldn't make their meeting. When she checked her phone at ten thirty, she had eleven missed calls and seven text messages. Susan was petrified. Nobody knew where Amanda was, and nobody had heard from Sam. It had turned into a Sheridan-wide hunt.

Amanda stepped into the hall to call Susan. She couldn't bring herself to feel guilty. She'd run out of emotional strength.

Susan answered on the first ring. "Are you all right?" She sounded frantic.

"We're at the hospital," Amanda warbled. "Genevieve has a horrible fever. It went down a little, but we're not out of the woods yet."

"Oh, Amanda." Susan was on the edge of tears. "I'll be there in ten minutes."

Amanda leaned against the cool wall of the hospital hallway and listened to the rest of the building's thwacks and beeps and heavy footsteps. The hospital felt like a mighty beast that had swallowed them up into this nightmare. It was a relief to know that Susan was on her way. She'd probably bring snacks. She'd make them drink water and force them to take a break. The world around Amanda looked blurry and strange. She'd walked through the looking glass.

Susan burst into the hospital room with a big backpack of Gatorade and water and sandwiches and sweets. Genevieve was crying, and Amanda and Sam were trying to calm her down while ensuring that her IV remained in. Susan touched Amanda's shoulder. Her eyes were bloodshot, as though she'd wept through the entire drive. There was nothing to say.

Genevieve finally went back to sleep twenty minutes later. Amanda, Sam, and Susan sat in the corner and spoke quietly as they ate their sandwiches. Susan knew to handle them with care and nod along as they explained more of the story. Sam and Amanda kept repeating the same parts, going in circles, but Susan never told them to stop. Amanda was so grateful. She tore open a package of Oreos and ate two at once.

Midway through her third Oreo, Amanda gasped and bolted to her feet. "What about the Arnouts?" she whispered.

Susan shook her head. "It doesn't matter right now."

Amanda turned to look at her infant daughter. She'd grown this baby in her womb for nearly ten months and loved her more than she'd ever loved anything. That included her career. It even included Sam.

Hardly loud enough for anyone else to hear, Amanda said, "I'll be there if her fever breaks." If and only if. And even then, she wasn't sure what she would do if she had to face the Arnouts after sleepless nights of terror. She couldn't imagine she would say only nice and considerate things. She couldn't imagine she'd behave.

Chapter Twenty-Five

Wes was in the shower when his phone rang. His gray hair was thick and curly with shampoo suds. As he reached to turn off the water, Beatrice called, "It's the historian! Want me to pick it up?"

"Yes, please!" Wes's heart thudded. He'd been expecting this call. He washed out his hair and stepped onto the rug to dry himself off, listening as Beatrice greeted the very first historian who'd come out to the Sunrise Cove after the construction workers' discovery: Dr. George Whitehead. He'd emailed Wes yesterday to say that he was on the verge of discovering "a great deal about Martha and Matthew Sheridan." He wanted to speak to him personally to disclose what he'd learned.

"He's just walking through the door," Beatrice said to Dr. Whitehead as Wes entered the living room in his robe. Beatrice's eyes were enormous as she passed over his cell.

"Hello, George. How are you?" Wes walked to the window and peered out at the sparkling June morning, hoping to calm himself. Ever since he'd begun the brand-new dementia medication, he'd had bouts of anxiety that made him feel he was losing control. Dr. Hamilton had said that was a normal side effect and nothing to be worried about—as long as the benefits outweighed the negative side effects.

"Morning, Wes. I'm sorry about my cryptic message yesterday. I was so wrapped up in research that I hardly pulled myself away to eat or sleep," George said.

"Is that right?" Wes laughed nervously.

"Your family history really sparked something in me. I feel like a young and hungry PhD student again," George said.

Wes's stomach twisted into knots. He knew better than to believe that that meant George had discovered only good news. Historians loved all kinds of stories, especially dark ones.

"Could I invite you and your wife to dinner tonight?" George asked. "I'm happy to meet you in Martha's Vineyard."

"We'll come to you," Wes suggested. Something about having George in the house he shared with Beatrice, discussing the intricacies of the Sheridan family's past, felt wrong to him. This house with Beatrice was his fresh start. No other Sheridan had ever lived here. It was untainted by the past.

George sent instructions to get to his place in a suburb of Boston. Beatrice was excited for a little trip, throwing snacks and drinks into a picnic basket and talking to herself and Wes without alerting him which dialogue was meant for whom. Wes put on a pair of slacks and a button-down and sat at the edge of the bed, thinking about the immensity of the day ahead. For reasons that he could only attribute to the medication, his thoughts felt sharper; he could follow his train of thought further than before. And when he took to his ledger to record what George had said, he recalled everything with startling accuracy.

"Beatrice?" Wes said, walking back through the living room to find her in the kitchen.

Beatrice stopped her frantic packing and peered up at him.

"I'm starting to notice a difference," he said quietly.

Beatrice knew exactly what he meant. She cleared the distance between them and threw her arms around his torso. She shook with tears, then mopped herself up and suggested they stay the night in Boston as the ferries were often awkwardly timed after dinner. She viewed it as a celebration, a night away. "A pre-wedding honeymoon." Wes agreed.

Wes retreated to the bedroom to pack a bag for the night. He considered what he'd learned last night about Amanda's baby. According to a text from Audrey this morning, Genevieve's fever had broken around midnight, thank goodness. It meant that Amanda would be allowed to represent herself in front of that wretched man's parents. The Arnouts. The people so sure of themselves and their goodness that they were willing to destroy anyone who doubted them. Wes checked the time and realized Susan and Amanda were about to enter court. He threw beautiful thoughts across the sound to the Nantucket Courthouse. He hoped they could feel his love.

Chapter Twenty-Six

From the Diary of Martha Smith
April 9, 1865

The war is over. The South has lost. The slaves are free.
  April 10, 1865
Yesterday, I was too ecstatic to write much more than that. Matthew came downstairs, flung open the trapdoor, and said, "It's time for you to live your life again." I picked up Mary and took her into the sunshine. God has never made a more beautiful day. Mary stretched her legs and sang her songs, then waddled up and down the beach in front of the Sheridan place. Her eyes were big and shining. The Sheridan children couldn't get enough of her: a new playmate. And I sat on the sand and wept into my hands. Eventually, I asked Matthew if I could borrow one of Wendy's bathing suits, and I waded into the freezing-cold water and raised my arms to the sky and felt more alive than I had since I was a child. Before I knew what it meant

to be a slave. Before I knew how entrapped I was. I imagined that I could feel the rapture of so many thousands of slaves across the country, discovering what freedom means for the first time. And I sang and danced and ran back up onto the sands to take Mary in my arms and cry.

Matthew made up a bed for Mary and me in the main house. It was the first time I slept above ground since our escape from Georgia.

Matthew and I woke up before the children this morning and went to the water. He asked me if I was thinking about heading north to find my sister and husband now that it was safe. I said of course, it was always on my mind. But Matthew told me he wasn't sure I should. "You don't know where they are; you have no way to make money; you have no community. If you stay here, I can help you." I wasn't sure what to make of it. My head was filled with questions. He said, "Ever since Wendy died, we've been like a ship without an anchor." I told him I know how to cook and clean; that I could teach his children to read and write. But I also told him that I wasn't planning on being a slave. I wanted days off sometimes. I wanted a wage. He smiled and agreed. I couldn't believe it! I had the strangest fear he was going to beat me instead.

April 16, 1865

An actor shot the president yesterday.

Matthew stopped me from running back downstairs in fear. He said, "The war is still over. The slaves are still free. But we have lost a great man." And we mourned together. It occurred to me that I am one of his only friends. And it's true that we've become quite close since we lost Wendy. We needed one another: me in the basement and him with four children and no wife.

What will the future hold? We have no leader. We are an aimless and broken nature. How will we heal?

July 11, 1865

This life is the most beautiful one I've ever known. The Sheridan children have taken Mary as one of their own. The girls dress her in their old gowns; the boys tease her and teach her games. I gather them all together for breakfast, lunch, and dinner—but mostly, they amuse themselves and watch out for each other. Mornings, I perform my chores and tidy the house, but afternoons are often for myself, for reading or writing or thinking. I've thought so often lately of Virgil and Jane, imagining where they ended up and what they think about the war ending. Sometimes I imagine them making a plan to come get me, but other times, I know I'm kidding myself. Sometimes I wonder if they really came, would I even want to go? I've grown so fond of the Vineyard Sound; of the sound of the waves; of the sparkling white beaches; of the fish that Matthew hauls in from a long day at sea for me to de-bone and fry up. We glow from eating fish and swimming in the sea. We glow from the hope that comes with the dawn after a horrible war.

October 16, 1865

I couldn't believe it when I walked out the door this morning. A harsh wind shot out from the sea and pummeled me. I nearly turned around to run back inside. But that's when I heard the sound of my name. A carriage grew closer. At the front of it were two colored people, a man and a woman. My heart surged. I pulled up my skirts and raced across the yard. I felt like a little girl again. By the time I reached them, my sister had leaped down and opened her arms for me. I fell into her and sobbed. She cried just as hard.

She smells different, like fine soap and lavender rather than Georgian fields and sorrow and rage. She looks beautiful and well-fed. She says my name over and over, as though she can't get enough.

The man with her is her husband, Jefferson. She met him in Canada, and they want to stay.

She tells me that every letter she sent here must never have made it. That she wrote and wrote herself to death only to never hear from me.

"I thought you were dead," she won't stop saying. "But I told Jefferson we had to come here and see for ourselves. And you're not dead! And Mary is the most gorgeous sight I've ever seen!"

Matthew agreed to let them stay for a few nights, which means we have a full house. I know that once night comes, I'll have to take Jane outside and ask her what happened to Virgil. I have a feeling I won't like the answer.

Later:

Jane and I just walked along the water beneath a pregnant orange moon. She told me the entire story of what happened after she and Virgil left me behind. It's brief.

After Martha's Vineyard, Jane and Virgil went north to another house outside of Boston and then another even farther north of that. That's as far as they got. They woke up in the middle of the night to gunshots. There was an uproar upstairs. Virgil was sure they would be found out. He tried to convince Jane to pack up and come with him immediately, but Jane was too frightened. "It sounded like they had the house surrounded," Jane told me. Jane stayed hidden in the tiny closet that served as the Underground Railroad hiding place while Virgil snuck out.

But Jane doesn't think he made it far. There was

another gunshot, followed by someone calling, "I got him! I got him!"

My heart sank as she told me this story. I remember my strong and quiet Virgil; remember that he's the father of my Mary; remember that when we first plotted to escape, it was Virgil who pushed hardest for us to go. Without him, Jane and I wouldn't be here on Martha's Vineyard.

I asked Jane what happened after that. How did she go on? She got lucky, she said. She met another group on the Railroad the next night, and they adopted her. They made it all the way to Canada, where she met Jefferson and got married. They have a house of their own, apparently. They're going to have a baby. They're going to have a normal life.

Jane keeps apologizing for leaving me behind. For heading north without me. But I keep pointing out the sky and the house and the five children in my care. I keep telling her about Matthew's goodness. I wouldn't have had any of it if she and Virgil hadn't packed up and left that night.

October 17, 1865

Jane pulled me aside this afternoon and warned me not to fall in love with Matthew. "It's better if you call him Mr. Sheridan," she said. "He's your boss." I told her that he pays me a wage and that I can take off time whenever I want. I told her that I'm not in love with him. I didn't tell her that I don't exactly know what "love" is anymore. That I feel damaged on the inside after losing Virgil and Wendy.

Jane told me that she heard talk about me in the village. That people speculate about my relationship with Matthew.

"*Don't forget that he's a white man in a white man's world*," she warned. "*Neither of you can escape that. The white man's world goes on forever, even into Canada.*"

I know she's right.

Chapter Twenty-Seven

Amanda, Susan, and Bruce Holland entered the Nantucket Courthouse at eleven sharp and sat on the right-hand side of the ornate hall. The pews and the judge's desk were made of shining mahogany. It felt slightly more like a church than a place of law and order. Furtively, she checked her phone for news about Genevieve from Sam—if her fever came back or the doctor said anything terrifying, Amanda was prepared to jump up and flee the courthouse. She was prepared to swim back to Martha's Vineyard if she had to.

But all Sam had written was: *Everything is great here! Genevieve is sleeping like a champ, and the nurses are celebrating her vital signs. Genevieve and I are pulling for you! We love you.*

Amanda blinked back tears and shoved her phone into her purse. The double-wide doors behind them opened to reveal Mr. and Mrs. Arnout along with their lawyer, Mary-Beth Walker, who was widely known among the legal community to work only with clients who could pay her four times the going rate. Her face had changed remarkably over the years as her pay rate had increased, so much so that her jawline was completely restructured, and her eyebrows made her look perpetually surprised. Still, she was gorgeous—and mean. She played dirty.

Amanda had hardly slept all week. She raised her chin and told herself a story about how alert she was. About how assertive she was. She wasn't going to take this abuse a moment longer. As though God was playing a joke on her, she immediately had to suppress a yawn.

As was customary, Mary-Beth Walker started the festivities with an opening statement. She spoke of the "gross misjustice" that had occurred due to the mishandling of Hilton Arnout's case. She spoke of what a "sterling member of his community" Hilton had been prior to his untimely arrest. And she brought up many details about Amanda's state of mind during the trial—namely her pregnancy—that, in her opinion, had contributed to Amanda's "horrific representation of Hilton Arnout and, beyond that, defamation of the entire Arnout family." According to Amanda's mother, the Arnouts sought damages of around three million dollars—which was laughable. It was nothing to the Arnouts and everything to Amanda. She was at the beginning of her life and counted every penny.

"It is our opinion that Ms. Harris should not work again," Mary-Beth Walker said. "Because Susan Sheridan and Bruce Holland assisted Ms. Harris in representing Hilton Arnout, it's our opinion that the court take a look at the law office to ensure they uphold Massachusetts law. Our goal is to ensure that Amanda Harris does not work another day as a lawyer for the State of Massachusetts—

and to ensure that all damages have been paid in order to protect the Arnout name."

Amanda focused on her breath through the opening statements. Her hands were in fists. This trial was a reminder of the reason she occasionally—very occasionally—hated American law. There were so many loopholes. It was a strange game you could manipulate for your own gain.

It was Susan's turn to give an opening statement. Amanda had watched her mother glide across the courtroom hundreds of times, delivering a narrative that suited the criminal she wanted to represent—one that demanded empathy for a system that so often wronged people of lesser incomes or addicts. But Hilton Arnout hadn't been an addict. He'd been given every opportunity to succeed —and he'd made a mockery of everyone who'd given him a leg-up. Now he was even making a mockery of Amanda from behind bars. It was incredible what money made you capable of. It made you immortal, practically.

Amanda's mouth tasted like cotton balls. She blinked away black spots that hovered in her vision. Susan cleared her throat and tapped the tips of her fingers together in preparation for her speech. But Amanda was suddenly struck with the realization that she didn't want her mother to fight this battle for her. Amanda was a mother now—a powerful creature who'd already been through the trauma of childbirth and the ache of watching her baby in the emergency room. The Arnouts were nothing but gum on her shoe. They needed to be removed.

Amanda was on her feet, gesturing for her mother to return to her seat. A moment of confusion passed over Susan's face, but she swept back as though this were all a part of the plan.

"Ms. Harris, Ms. Sheridan? Let's proceed," the judge said.

Amanda passed her mother and found herself between the judge and the Arnouts. She took her mother's traditional stance with her fingertips pressed together and her heart in her throat. For a second, she made eye contact with Mrs. Arnout, then Mr. Arnout, thinking of what it had been like for them to raise Hilton from birth and learn that he'd committed such an egregious act. They were willing to fight tooth and nail for it not to be so in a court of law. But that didn't make it go away. Not really.

At this point in Amanda's career, she'd done upward of thirty opening statements by herself. Every case required a different tactic, a different attack. But, at its core, the Arnouts' anger came from love and confusion. It came from sorrow at their own failure.

Amanda hadn't rehearsed this. She wavered from foot to foot.

"I want to start by saying that you're right about one thing," Amanda said. "I am relatively inexperienced. A little bit younger than your son, in fact, and just about a year out of law school. But that doesn't mean I don't know what I'm doing." Amanda set her jaw. She could feel her mother's eyes boring holes into her. "I graduated at the top of my class in law school. I have fought valiantly for upward of thirty clients. And I grew up with a mother and father who fought for thousands of their own clients over the years. Criminals—or not—who needed their help during times of strife."

Mr. and Mrs. Arnout were not accustomed to being spoken to so directly in an official court of law. They squirmed and glanced at one another as though they wanted to ask if this was allowed. In fact, Amanda wouldn't have been surprised if the judge interrupted her and told her to address him rather than the Arnouts. But she proceeded until then.

"I've just become a mother," Amanda said. "I suppose you know this, as you've decided to use the fact that I was pregnant last year as one of the reasons I couldn't support your son as well as he needed. I find this astounding, especially coming from another mother." Amanda locked eyes with Mrs. Arnout and felt a surge of emotion. She was almost sure that Mrs. Arnout was on the brink of tears. More than that, she was sure that Mr. Arnout couldn't fathom what it meant to love a child so much that you couldn't sleep when they couldn't sleep; that you felt their physical aches just as painfully; that you were willing to lay down your life for them if only to ensure they made it one more day.

In fact, she felt sure Mr. Arnout was angrier about the defamation of the Arnout name rather than his son's time in prison.

"Since I became a mother," Amanda said, "I've experienced a great deal of empathy for your situation, Mr. and Mrs. Arnout. The idea that my daughter would grow up and break the law or hurt anyone is a horrible thing to carry. But it leads me to a legal issue. One that is rather difficult to face. When we turn eighteen, those of us who are mentally and emotionally sound are self-sufficient in a court of law. It is up to us to sustain ourselves; to contribute to society; to become the sort of people who would make our parents proud. As you all know, my mother and father are both criminal defense lawyers. I wanted to be just like them when I grew up. And hopefully I've gotten close."

Amanda swallowed. She hoped she was making sense. Her thoughts rattled around her brain.

"If I committed a heinous crime tomorrow," Amanda said, "the world would necessarily look down on me and deal with me as they saw fit. By extension, they would look down on my mother, too. I would feel tremendous guilt for that. But I would know that the crime was mine. Not my mother's. Not my father's.

"A jury of twelve listened to the evidence against Hilton Arnout. They declared him guilty, and I do not object to their findings. Neither did Hilton. His parents are the only people dragging this out further than it needs to go. And I know they're partially doing it out of love. Out of guilt. Out of not wanting to admit to themselves that their son was capable of something like this. But as a new mother who knows how fragile the world and our relationships truly are, I ask you: is it worth it? Is it worth it to drag this out even further, force Hilton's name back in everyone's minds, and face a judge based on only your 'feelings' about something? I know that the Arnouts have the governor and numerous other people in their pockets. I know they are very powerful. But I hope the judge will take into account the fact that my mother, Bruce Holland, and I work diligently to ensure we never go beyond the limits of the law. Our law office must be safe against people like the Arnouts. And my career should withstand what is genuinely a tantrum about how things should have gone."

Mrs. Arnout was on her feet. For a moment, Amanda thought she was going to storm toward her and smack her on the face. The "tantrum" line was way too far; Amanda knew she was out of line. But Mrs. Arnout burst down the aisle and disappeared through the double-wide doors. Mr.

Arnout glowered at Amanda and followed her. Their prosecutor got to her feet and smiled demurely at the judge. Amanda had the sense that Mary-Beth Walker wanted to rip her apart.

The judge was flummoxed. "I suppose we'll take a recess until the prosecution returns." He tapped the gavel.

Amanda, Susan, and Bruce gathered their things and walked to the back chambers to wait. Bruce's wife, Elsa, came with them, whispering to Bruce so quietly that Amanda couldn't eavesdrop. Amanda swam between fear that she'd just done something incredibly stupid and excitement that she'd done something really incredible. When the chamber door closed, Susan looked at Amanda, puffed out her cheeks, and said, "That was brave. Maybe it was stupid, but it was brave."

Amanda placed her hand over her mouth and shook with nervous laughter. "I got carried away."

Susan pulled her hair into a ponytail that she immediately let drop. "I doubt that anyone has spoken so firmly to the Arnouts before. Regardless of what happens after this, you should see that as a win." She collapsed on a chair and hung her head and chuckled. "Oh, Amanda. I don't know what to say."

"I'm exhausted," Amanda said.

Amanda went down the hall to fetch them cups of coffee and stretch her legs. June sunlight filtered through the dirty windows of the courthouse, and she could hear the birds chirping. She imagined herself a year from now with toddler Genevieve, walking through a sun-drenched path. She imagined herself telling Genevieve all the birds' names. She made a mental note to ask her grandfather more about that. He was the expert.

When Amanda returned to the chambers, the judge was chatting with her mother as though they'd known one another for years. It turned out they had. He'd gone to school with Richard and Susan back in the day and had even been invited to their wedding but hadn't been able to attend. "I was sorry to hear about you and Richard," he said, to which Susan responded, "Don't be. I'm happier than ever right now."

The judge didn't wait long to explain what had happened. Mrs. Arnout was so upset after Amanda's opening statement that she ran to the harbor and hired a fishing boat to take her around the island to the Arnout estate. "I don't think she wanted to be in a car with Mr. Arnout," the judge explained. "Mr. Arnout stormed back to the courthouse with the idea that he wanted to continue the trial, but as he spoke to Mary-Beth about getting back in there, Mrs. Arnout called and said she would divorce him if he kept this 'silly lawsuit going.' That's what I overheard."

Amanda's jaw dropped. She'd been right to assume that the full brunt of this attack had been from Mr. Arnout's side. She imagined Mrs. Arnout out on a fishing boat in the sunshine, her perfectly blown-out hair disintegrating in the sea winds. She imagined Mrs. Arnout taking a trip to see her son very soon so that she could hold his hand, look him in the eye, and say, "You did a bad thing. But that doesn't mean I love you any less."

That was what Susan would have done if Amanda committed a crime. And it was what Amanda would do with Genevieve, too. Because that sort of love was messy and chaotic, and it made people do terrible and insane things. But that sort of love never faded, either. It was foolproof.

Chapter Twenty-Eight

Wes and Beatrice reached Dr. George Whitehead's home in the suburbs of Boston at seven o'clock that evening. It was a red-brick colonial with a mailbox shaped like a cardinal. "A fellow birder!" Beatrice suggested as she cut the engine. Before they reached the front stoop, George opened the door wearing an apron covered in flour. "Apologies! I'm making my own pasta," he said. "It's a little bit of a mess. But I figured it was worth a shot."

George led them into the kitchen, where dinner was prepared, and a bottle of wine was airing out. George's wife, Karen, stood to shake their hands and thank them for coming all this way.

"We wanted to get off the island," Wes said. "We've been cooped up there all winter long."

"George was just telling me you have a wedding coming up," Karen said. "How exciting!"

"Not long now," Beatrice admitted. "But everything has fallen into place. We just have to show up."

The four of them sat down to dinner. Wes felt

jittery about what George would reveal about his family's past, but he tried to stay in the moment. Karen discussed her work in the city's arts council, and George talked about a newly discovered historical site outside of Providence. When Beatrice brought up the cardinal mailbox, Karen gushed with stories about their recent birding adventures in Scotland, and Beatrice suggested they all go birding together sometime. Wes watched her, mystified. Socializing was so easy for her. She slipped easily into any sort of company and any conversation.

After dinner, Karen suggested dessert, but Wes was too jittery.

"I think it's time," George said, guiding them to his study.

George's study looked like something outside of time. Enormous gold-plaited frames hung paintings from the seventeenth and eighteenth centuries; books lined nearly every wall; and he had two computers, a typewriter, and what looked to be hundreds of old notebooks. "I write everything down," he said, "and then have to type everything up again. I love the old typewriter, but I'm afraid it's not very practical these days."

A glass box in the corner of the room protected Martha's diary. Wes gazed down upon it, his fingers itchy. He wanted to pick it up and leaf through it, but he knew the paper was too fragile and would all come apart in his hands.

"It's truly an extraordinary piece," George said quietly.

"Quentin said the diary ends after she learns she's pregnant," Wes remembered. He was again struck with how easily he'd recalled that. "I've been dying to know what happened. If she stayed? Moved away? And what happened to her daughter?"

George gave him a soft smile that meant he'd learned everything. He sat at his desk and gestured for Wes and Beatrice to sit across from him.

"I'm friendly with a retired historian who lives on Nantucket Island," he began. "He's documented hundreds of letters, diaries, and photographs of Martha's Vineyard and Nantucket from 1860 to 1880. I told him about Martha and the Sheridans and asked if anything in his extensive research had clued him in about what had happened. It took him more than a week to go through his organized files. But he found something that fit together well with Martha's journal entries.

"Back in 1867, Matthew Sheridan was a thirty-two-year-old widower with four children. That's quite young by today's standards, of course. And the women on Martha's Vineyard seemed to think so, too.

"My historian friend clued me in to a correspondence between a woman named Clarice and her daughter Nelly. Nelly was living in Boston as a young woman, and Clarice was trying everything to get Nelly to return to Martha's Vineyard and start a family. Records indicate that Nelly was writing articles for a local paper in Boston at the time, which was a startling feat for a young woman back then.

"Clarice really liked Matthew Sheridan. He lived three properties away from where she'd raised Nelly and her boys, and she was friendly with all of the Sheridan children and even, for a while, Martha. She wrote about Martha in her letters to Nelly, explaining how strange it was that Martha had had to live in the basement all that time. Here's a quote: *'Martha seems just the same as the* rest of us. *She just wants to care for her baby. She just wants her husband by her side.'* It seems likely that Clarice was trying to use Martha's plight as a way to guilt Nelly into returning.

"But in 1886, the letters change. She started begging Nelly to return home to 'save' Matthew from himself. Between Martha's diary and Clarice's letters, it's clear that Martha and Matthew had fallen in love. This caused a great deal of pain for Martha. She didn't want anyone on the island to know, because she was sure they would 'chase her away.' She was still Black in a predominantly White society. But Clarice was around too often. She saw right through them and started to spread rumors. Nobody believed it at first. But when Martha ended up pregnant in 1887, the island of Martha's Vineyard created a hostile environment for Martha, Matthew, and their five children. Martha never writes down what she and Matthew discussed during this time. It's not clear if he asked her to leave or if she left of her own accord. What is clear, however, is that she left Martha's Vineyard when she was three or four months pregnant and traveled north to Canada to live with her sister."

George grabbed his phone to show on the map where the Canadian village was located just sixty miles north of the United States-Canada border. Wes's hands were in fists. He was struggling not to cry.

"I contacted the village—it's called Forrester—and asked if they had any records of ex-slaves who'd come there during 1887. Apparently, they had a wonderful recordkeeper at that time. They even had photographs!"

George searched through his laminated files to pull out a grainy old photograph of a beautiful and fierce-looking Black woman. She was pregnant and carried a toddler on her hip. She looked as though she wore the weight of the world on her shoulders, but she was strong enough to take it.

Wes's eyes filled with tears. The baby in her womb was his great-grandfather's brother or sister. They'd been forced out of the original Sheridan House—away from their lineage and their beautiful island home. Because of racism. Because of the horrors of a long-ago country.

Beatrice touched his wrist. This was a lot to take in.

"Go on," Wes urged George. "I want to know everything."

George put down the photograph of pregnant Martha and Mary and folded his hands. "Martha gave birth to a boy that autumn. She named him Sheridan Smith."

"Sheridan!" Wes cried. He couldn't believe it.

"Sheridan went on to find a printing press company in 1891," George said, showing him a laminated newspaper article that featured a photograph of Sheridan with his arms crossed, standing in front of his newly founded company. He wore a wide-brimmed hat that had been in fashion at the time. "He married a young Black woman named Sara and had five children. It's difficult after that to see where all of the Sheridan-Smiths ended up. Some of them came to America; one traveled to Australia and was never heard from again. Others stayed in Canada. Here's a genealogical tree for you," George said, passing it over the desk. "But I don't know if it's of any interest."

Wes read the tree slowly: names and birthplaces and death places he'd never once heard of. Wes Sheridan had always assumed he knew everything about the Sheridan family line. But this was a branch—or, rather, an enormous tree—that he hadn't accounted for. His hands shook.

At the top was the name Martha Smith. She'd died of old age at ninety-two. Wes pictured her surrounded by friends and family who loved her. He imagined her so far away from that basement that it seemed like a bad dream.

"What happened to Matthew?" Beatrice asked.

"I believe he died in 1893," George said. "He never remarried. After most of his children had gone, he built onto the house and made it into a bed-and-breakfast for those who visited the island. You could say that he was the one who put hospitality in the Sheridan blood."

That night, Wes gathered everything George had copied for him on the hotel desk and gave it a second and third look. He gazed intently into Martha's eyes, looking for clues. He read over snippets of her diary to get a sense of her personality. He was blown over by her poetic language and her will to live.

Beatrice approached him from behind and kissed him on the back of the neck. A shiver ran down his spine.

Wes turned to look her in the eyes. Everything felt so tremendously heavy. Sometimes he asked himself why were they going through with this wedding? They were old. They had already been through so much. So many people had come before them and struggled and tried and eventually passed on.

Somehow, Beatrice understood. She took his hands in hers and said, "It's our job to keep going for them."

How did she always know exactly what to say?

Wes and Beatrice slept peacefully in the thousand-count sheets of the hotel bed beneath the same moon that had led Martha to freedom so many years before. Wes did not wake up with nightmares. He didn't dream at all.

Chapter Twenty-Nine

It was incredible how quickly Amanda's law license was restored. The Massachusetts Board of Bar Overseers contacted her in early July to declare they'd reviewed her case and decided she was a lawyer of sound mind and principles. They wished her well. Amanda considered framing the letter but thought better of it and threw it in the recycling. She was happy to put this period of her life behind her.

"It was never your fault," her mother assured her over a congratulatory dinner that night.

But Amanda thought she'd learned a great lesson throughout that process. Number one: moneyed people could hurt you if you let them. Number two: when it came down to it, Amanda could live without her career. Her long and sun-dappled days with Genevieve and Sam were enough. God forbid, if she ever lost her law license again, she would find another way to survive. She would use her intellect some other way. She would teach or write or help Sam at the inn. She would always be

Amanda Harris with a unique set of skills that would serve her well in whatever field she chose.

All at once, it was the Friday before Grandpa Wes's wedding to Beatrice. Time had really had its way with them. Before long, it would be autumn.

Amanda met Audrey for a walk on the trail between the Sheridan House and the Sunrise Cove. Max was with his grandmother Lola, and Amanda had Genevieve in a carrier on her back, where she slept soundly as they padded along. July sunlight splintered the bright green and lush tops of trees. Everything looked taken from a dream. Audrey was talking about another journalistic case she was trying to break, something about a Boston hotel with a seedy underbelly. Amanda knew Audrey would figure out what was afoot. But she begged her to take care of herself along the way. "You don't know what dangerous people lurk behind this story. Keep your wits about you."

Audrey said she would, then teased, "You're the big sister I never had."

Amanda's heart swelled. As a little kid, she wanted a girl cousin or a sister—somebody to share her secrets with. She'd adored her brother and still did, but he'd never fit the bill.

"What are you wearing tonight again?" Audrey asked as she tied her hair into a high ponytail. Her elbows were pointy, her upper arms tan.

"That dress you helped me pick out in Manhattan," Amanda said. "You?"

"I'll probably steal something from my mom's closet," Audrey said. "Like always."

Tonight was the rehearsal dinner for Wes and Beatrice in the Aquinnah Cliffside Overlook Hotel—a perfect place for a wedding and the same venue where Amanda had married Sam last summer. Her wedding had been topsy-turvy—complete with a mid-wedding thief and a whole lot of confusion about where the groom had gone. She hoped Grandpa's wedding would prove to be a bit calmer.

They rounded the last bend of the trail, and the Sunrise Cove Inn came into view. Amanda stopped for a moment to take a breath. She never tired of looking at that beautiful inn: the beating heart of her family and the place that tied them all together. As they approached, Sam and Grandpa Wes came out to speak to a number of reporters, all of whom waved microphones in their faces. Today was the first day of the Sunrise Cove's reopening. Excitement for the basement room and its place in history had activated a rush of tourism that would carry them all the way into winter 2025. Sam practically floated these days. He thanked Amanda continually. "If you hadn't come up with that plan to save the Cove, we would have had to close our doors forever."

Not many men went out of their way to thank their wives the way Sam did. Amanda always remembered to count her blessings.

When the reporters faded away and left Sam and Grandpa Wes alone, Amanda and Audrey approached. Grandpa gushed with excitement. "Look at this place, girls! Back up and running, just like always! Zach's inside cooking up a storm for lunch, and Christine made a huge batch of scones. They're delicious. In fact, I might have another one."

Amanda had noticed a tremendous shift in Grandpa's moods and memory the past few weeks. The rumor was he was on a new medication—one that removed the plaque on his neurons and kept his memory alive a little while longer. It was never clear to Amanda how long they'd have him; how long it would be till everything was thrown off its axis. But she smiled wider as he spoke with his hands, telling them about all the chaos at the Sunrise Cove from the past few days. Sam had already told her, of course. But she wanted to give Grandpa Wes as much time to speak as he pleased.

In the foyer, Grandpa Wes had hung a beautiful portrait of Martha. The photograph had been discovered after the others, in a hidden cabinet in the old basement room. It seemed likely that Matthew had wanted to hide that period of his life away. Perhaps his love for Martha hurt him too much after she'd gone. Perhaps he'd hated himself for letting her go.

Matthew's involvement in why Martha had gone away was lost to time. It was clear he was the father of her baby, and this wouldn't have been cause for celebration across Martha's Vineyard. Amanda knew it was devastating to Grandpa Wes to consider the fact that Matthew had been the one to send Martha on her way. *People made mistakes*, she wanted to remind him. But there was no rewriting the past.

Martha smiled in the photo, a rare thing to see in those days. Beside her on the grass was her toddler daughter, Mary. Yonder in the yard were two of the four Sheridan children, scampering barefoot. It looked like a blissful summer day on Martha's Vineyard—not unlike today. The more things changed, the more they stayed the same.

Amanda imagined the last decades of Martha's and Mary's lives in Canada. She imagined Martha bringing Sheridan Smith into the world, teaching him to read, write, and appreciate the freedom he'd always known. She imagined the pride Martha had had when her son founded his own printing press company—proving himself to be just as well-read as any fully White man.

Christine appeared with a platter of blueberry scones. Her face was pink from the heat of the kitchen. From down the hall came Zach's voice as he called out to one of his sous chefs. A stream of tourists entered the bistro and filled the tables, eager to dine at one of the best establishments across the island.

Amanda took a scone and took a big bite. Christine watched expectantly. No matter how good she knew she was, she always needed to hear it.

"These are delicious, Aunt Christine!" Amanda cried.

"So good," Audrey agreed.

Christine looked euphoric. "It's so good to be back in the kitchen together," she said, peering down the hall at Zach as he burst out of the kitchen door to help a server set another table. "Zach is just as stressed as ever."

"You sound wistful," Audrey joked.

"Zach and I don't know what to do with ourselves when we don't have stress from the bistro," she explained. "It's a part of our genetic makeup at this point. Mia is doomed."

Audrey, Amanda, Grandpa Wes, and Christine laughed together as still more tourists buzzed past them. Some paused briefly to look at Martha's photograph on the wall. A woman said, "That was the ex-slave who lived downstairs. I heard on NPR she had a Sheridan baby and went north."

Amanda realized it was a story that would be exchanged for generations to come. Perhaps one day—a hundred years from now—a Sheridan child would tell stories about Amanda, Sam, and Genevieve. Maybe they would see them as part of the dense texture of this old and iconic place. She and Martha would be long gone yet immortal.

* * *

Audrey, Lola, Christine, Amanda, and Susan met at the Sheridan House later that day to get ready for the rehearsal dinner. It felt just like old times: running from one end of the house to the other to ask opinions about makeup and hair and outfits. Max squelched with excitement every time Audrey passed him by. Amanda was ready before everyone else—as usual—and nibbling on a cucumber as Genevieve slept in her carrier. She'd considered getting a babysitter for the first time but still didn't like the thought of leaving Genevieve with a stranger. That would come later, she guessed. When she went back to work in two weeks. When things inevitably changed, and she was given the dynamic blessing of watching her daughter grow out of her baby clothes and into her childhood and then into adulthood. When she was given the blessing of watching time go by.

Sam sent a selfie of himself and Noah in their suits. Noah had his tongue sticking out. Amanda showed the photo to Audrey as she buzzed past, and Audrey said, "What a nerd!" But she said it with all the love in her heart.

Susan drove Amanda and Genevieve to the Aquinnah Cliffside that night. As soon as Amanda got out of the car, Sam rushed across the parking lot to take Genevieve's carrier and kiss her. This hotel was their special place, and they'd just celebrated their one-year anniversary—an event that had failed miserably because Genevieve had had an ear infection and Sam had had to meet with a building inspector for the Sunrise Cove. But they'd made popcorn, watched a movie, and called each other "old." They were over the moon in love. And that meant enjoying the practicality of wearing their pajamas as they celebrated, sometimes.

There was nobody she would rather get old with.

The rehearsal mostly went off without a hitch. Charlotte, the wedding planner, flowed easily through the Sheridans, telling everyone where to stand, where to walk, and where to sit. Max was the ringbearer, and he handled his role as diligently as any three-year-old could have before bursting into tears and holding Audrey's legs. "He'll be fine tomorrow," she promised. "He's just tired." By the end of the hour, he was passed out upstairs in an empty guest room, where Genevieve slept peacefully in a crib. Amanda held the baby monitor as she and Audrey grabbed drinks at the bar and scouted for their name tags for dinner. Smells of seafood and Cajun spices came from the kitchen, and Amanda's stomach gurgled with hunger.

Audrey, Noah, Amanda, Sam, Aunt Kelli's daughter Lexi, Isabella, and Isabella's boyfriend Rhett sat at a round table near the window. Servers frequently came by to refill their wine and water glasses, and their conversations were boisterous. Isabella and Rhett were talking about a sailing trip they'd just taken with friends of theirs, Cole and Aria. Cole was one of the top sailors in the district. Tommy Gasbarro often called him "his only real rival on the island," which was saying something.

"You're so adventurous," Amanda said, balancing her chin on her fist and stifling a yawn.

Isabella laughed. "You're the one who had a baby. That's the bravest thing of all."

Lexi nodded vigorously and took a bite of salmon. "Give me a sailing trip any day of the week. Give me a stormy sea! Having a baby sounds terrifying by comparison."

Amanda laughed and exchanged a glance with Audrey. They both understood the tremendous pain and adrenaline and exhaustion and ache that came with motherhood. But they knew it came with once-in-a-lifetime joys and a nuanced understanding and empathy for the world around them. More than that, they knew they couldn't possibly translate this to anyone who hadn't gone through it themselves.

Grandpa Wes stood between dinner and dessert to give a speech. His eyes were as clear as crystal as he raised his glass. The Sheridan-Montgomery families and all Martha's Vineyard friends—plus a few from Nantucket— quieted and turned to look at him.

"I want to thank you for coming out tonight to celebrate my love and me," Grandpa Wes said, touching Beatrice's shoulder. Beatrice blushed. Her eyes glinted with tears. "Needless to say, it's been a tremendously different sort of spring and summer for us Sheridans. I grew up at the Sunrise Cove. I grew up watching my mother and father work the books, greet guests, clean bistro tables, and wake up early to do it all over again. I never knew anything but that life and was proud to do it all my working life. The fact that secrets lurked under my feet the entire time still startles me. But it's given me a wonderful context and comprehension of the Sheridan family past. We Sheridans are a result of generations of kindness and loyalty and love. And it brings me enormous joy to know that that love will be celebrated here tonight and tomorrow when I wed Beatrice. It's the sort of love that will reverberate through the next generations and the ones after that. I know that my great-great-great-grand-children will feel the love I have in my heart today—so long after I am gone." Grandpa Wes's voice broke as he raised his glass. "To love."

The crowd echoed, "To love."

Chapter Thirty

No disease could destroy Wes's memory of his first wedding—not even the all-powerful dementia. Images of that long-ago day were drilled into him—Anna walking toward him in a glowing white dress; his father getting weepy-eyed as he gave a speech about commitment and the power of family; his mother trying to clean up after everyone, even in the middle of the reception as a way to feel useful and distract herself from her emotions. He'd slow-danced with Anna all night long and into the morning, whispering into her ear, "I'll love you till the day I die, Anna Banana. That's a promise. And Wes Sheridan has never told a lie."

It was true that Wes still loved Anna deep in his bones. But it was also true that on July 6, 2024, he stood before one hundred of his family members and dearest friends before the splendor of the Aquinnah Cliffside Overlook Hotel, preparing to marry Beatrice—a woman beyond his wildest dreams. A woman who accepted him for who he was right now at the age of seventy-three. A woman prepared to take him and the plaque in his brain and his wrinkles and his bad knees and all. A woman who so often said, "Wes Sheridan, sometimes I think I dreamed you up."

It was remarkable to do that here at the Aquinnah Cliffside Overlook Hotel. It was where his parents had met back in the forties—when his mother had been married to someone else. His parents had had to fight everything, including a violent hurricane, to be together. It was only because of their love that he was here.

There wasn't a dry eye across the lawn as Beatrice walked up the aisle arm in arm with Tommy Gasbarro. Even manly Tommy's chin wiggled. Apparently, his fears for Wes's health had waned. He just wanted Wes and Beatrice to have a lovely life together. He wanted everyone to have the kind of tenderness and support he and Lola had together in their little cabin in the woods.

Beatrice was a knock-out. Her cream-colored gown was simple and classic, like something out of the forties. Wes had been told his tuxedo had a remarkable cut. "Your style is outstanding these days, Grandpa," Amanda had said many times.

A pastor Wes had known forever joined Wes and Beatrice in holy matrimony. He said everything the way it was meant to be richer or poorer; in sickness and in health; all the days of your life. And Wes kissed Beatrice with his eyes closed and knew in his heart of hearts he would never forget this day. Even on his deathbed, he would recount it back to himself.

Charlotte had done a marvelous job of planning the wedding. This was no surprise. Wes felt as though he floated through the festivities. He kissed his sister Kerry on the cheek and shook Trevor's hand wildly. He sipped small amounts of champagne—never too much. And he never strayed far from Beatrice, who looked seventy going on twenty-five, such was the energy of her joy. Over and over again, she showed off her rings and her stylish hairpiece. She spoke of the honeymoon they'd planned—one to Jamaica, a place Wes had never dreamed of going. Beatrice had shown him photographs of the birds they had down there. She'd even gotten him a pair of new binoculars as a pre-wedding present.

That night, as the stars spackled the night sky, the band Charlotte had hired played an inspired rendition of "Moon River" as Beatrice and Wes swayed.

"I keep wanting to say something," Wes told her tenderly, touching the tip of his nose to hers. "Something important. Something that will crystallize this moment in time."

Beatrice shook her head ever so slightly. "You don't need to say anything at all. Let's just live in it."

As the song drifted out to bring in the more upbeat track of "Pennsylvania 6-9000," Wes turned as Amanda and Audrey swarmed him with hugs and happy smiles. Just as they had all those days at the Sheridan House, they cackled and danced, moving their hips and waving their hands. It reminded Wes of when Lola, Christine, and Susan had been girls dancing and jumping around to Michael Jackson in the living room. That was the thing about dancing: you did not think about getting old when you did it.

Grab the Salt Sisters

Dive into The Salt Sisters

Other Books by Katie Winters

The Vineyard Sunset Series

Secrets of Mackinac Island Series

Sisters of Edgartown Series

A Katama Bay Series

A Mount Desert Island Series

A Nantucket Sunset Series

The Coleman Series

The Salt Sisters

The Sutton Book Club

A Frosty Season Series